"Put This On," He Said. Lifting The Large Solitaire With A Diamond-Studded Band, He Caught Her Left Hand And Pushed The Ring Onto Her Finger.

Gwen gaped at the ring, shocked at how well it fit. "How did you know—"

"Pretend you're madly in love with me," he said and tugged her toward the front door.

"But what—"

"The paparazzi," he said and opened the door.

Gwen immediately heard a dozen clicks from the camera. Luc slid his arm around her waist. "Gotta give you guys credit. You're the first. You make it damn hard to keep a relationship private."

He turned toward Gwen and dipped his head. "I think they've caught us, sweetheart," he said and lowered his mouth to hers.

* * *

Don't miss an exclusive in-book short story by Maureen Child, available *only* in next month's HUDSONS OF BEVERLY HILLS title, *Tempted Into the Tycoon's Trap* by Emily McKay.

Dear Reader,

I'm so thrilled to launch this exciting, juicy series, THE HUDSONS OF BEVERLY HILLS! There's money and scandal and, most importantly, *great* men. In my story, shero Gwen McCord has left Hollywood eating her dust and she has no desire to return. She's happy where she is, but a family emergency and Luc Hudson force her to change plans. Luc turns her peaceful life upside down. We all want a man like that in our lives, yes?

If this juicy series weren't enough, we're also celebrating Harlequin's sixtieth birthday. Sixty years of emotional, satisfying stories filled with sheroes we want to be and heroes that make our hearts skip a beat.

Before I ever sold my first book, I dreamed of selling my books to Silhouette Desire. I loved the fact that I could count on the passion and emotional fulfillment in every story. Writing for Silhouette Desire is a dream come true. Every day I'm privileged to weave a story featuring a heart-stopping, all-man hero and the lucky, deserving shero who teaches him the importance of love.

Here's to you, Harlequin Books, for all the excitement and pleasure you continue to bring us all!

Leanne Banks

LEANNE BANKS

BLACKMAILED INTO A FAKE ENGAGEMENT

Silhouette® Desire

Published by Silhouette Books
America's Publisher of Contemporary Romance

Special thanks and acknowledgments
to Leanne Banks for her contribution to
The Hudsons of Beverly Hills miniseries.

This book is dedicated to all the readers
and lovers of Harlequin Books and Silhouette Desire.

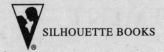 SILHOUETTE BOOKS

Recycling programs
for this product may
not exist in your area.

ISBN-13: 978-0-373-76916-2
ISBN-10:   0-373-76916-4

BLACKMAILED INTO A FAKE ENGAGEMENT

LEANNE BANKS

is a *New York Times* and *USA TODAY* bestselling author who is surprised every time she realizes how many books she has written. Leanne loves chocolate, the beach and new adventures. To name a few, Leanne has ridden on an elephant, stood on an ostrich egg (no, it didn't break), gone parasailing and indoor skydiving. Leanne loves writing romance because she believes in the power and magic of love. She lives in Virginia with her family and her four-and-a-half-pound Pomeranian, named Bijou.

THE HUDSONS OF BEVERLY HILLS

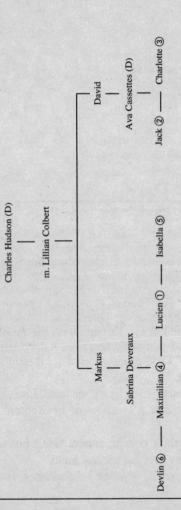

Charles Hudson (D)

m. Lillian Colbert

Markus

Sabrina Deveraux —— Lucien ① —— Isabella ⑤

David

Ava Cassettes (D) —— Charlotte ③

Jack ②

Devlin ⑥ —— Maximilian ④

KEY:
m: Married
D: Deceased
d: divorced
E: Engaged

① *Blackmailed Into a Fake Engagement* — January 2009
② *Tempted Into the Tycoon's Trap* — February 2009
③ *Transformed Into the Frenchman's Mistress* — March 2009
④ *Bargained Into Her Boss's Bed* — April 2009
⑤ *Propositioned Into a Foreign Affair* — May 2009
⑥ *Seduced Into a Paper Marriage* — June 2009

Prologue

"I bet my Ferrari," Devlin Hudson said to Luc in a room filled with cigar smoke, brotherly rivalries and the aroma of expensive alcohol.

"You sold your Ferrari," Luc said, calmly arranging the cards in his hand. "I bet my twenty-five-year-old scotch."

"Technicality," Devlin said, clamping his mouth over the cigar. "Check."

"Your cards must smell like your feet," Luc said.

Max Hudson took a swallow of his scotch. "I'm holding."

Jack Hudson, their cousin, swore. "He's not saying much. That means he's got a killer hand."

Jack was an excellent judge of character, but Luc

knew that Max could bluff with the best of them, even if he did it quietly. "That's what he wants you to believe."

Max slid Luc a sideways glance. "Your PR psychology has gone to your head."

"You wish," Luc said. "I see the dirty underbelly, and I usually know when someone is taking me for a ride."

Jack looked from Luc to Max. "I'll see your scotch and add my Patrón," he said.

"You're toast," Luc said.

"Shut up," Max said.

Devlin just growled.

Luc's cell phone rang, interrupting the game.

"Oh, no. Is this another of your young girlfriends?" Jack asked.

"He always goes for the young ones," Max said in agreement.

"The older ones know better," Dev added.

"Luc Hudson," he said into the phone.

"This is Officer Walker with the L.A.P.D. I'm calling on behalf of Miss Nicki McCord. She's being charged with driving under the influence and asked that we call you." The man cleared his throat. "She's not in the best shape at the moment."

Luc rose to his feet. "Where are you taking her?"

The officer gave the location. "Sir, she was driving the wrong way down a one-way street and narrowly missed hitting a family returning from a trip to Disneyland."

Luc raked his hand through his hair and shook his head. "I'll be there as soon as possible," he said and turned off the phone. "Sorry. Nicki McCord. I have to go."

"DUI, right?" Devlin said.

Luc nodded.

"Damn," Max said. "What are we going to do about the prepublicity for *The Waiting Room?* Nicki was supposed to start the PR jaunt next week."

"If only you were dealing with her sister Gwen instead," Jack said. "I hear she was a complete professional."

"Except when she left her ex-husband high and dry during their last movie," Devlin said.

"With Peter Horrigan, you don't know how much of that was spin or not."

Luc felt his mood turn grim. "I'm going to have to do some spinning of my own."

"You're the family problem solver," Devlin said. "Go do what you do best."

One

"**I**'m Luc Hudson. There's been an emergency with your sister, Nicki."

Gwen McCord's heart plunged into her stomach as she looked at the tall, handsome man with the watchful blue eyes standing on her front porch. She barely noticed her yellow Lab's barks over the panic racing through her. "Is she okay? Is she—" The worst possible thought stole the rest of her words and breath.

"She's alive," he said and nodded toward the door. "May I come in?"

"Yes, of course," Gwen said, pushing a strand of her hair behind her ear, stepping aside and pulling June, her dog, away from the doorway. Lost in her concern for Nicki, some part of her noticed the man's height and broad shoulders as he passed by her. He smelled of rich leather and just a hint of a spicy male scent. She glanced past him, spotting the SUV he'd driven to her ranch. For a member of one of Hollywood's most powerful families, the Hudsons, to make a personal visit to her in Montana, something terrible must have happened.

Gwen's stomach clenched in fear. "Please go ahead and tell me. Is she in the hospital?"

"No, we put her in rehab," Luc said, resting his hands on his hips. "She was arrested for driving drunk. Driving the wrong way on a one-way street. The police clocked her speeding thirty miles over the speed limit. She narrowly missed a head-on collision with a family of four returning from Disneyland."

"Oh my God," Gwen said, feeling her blood drop to her feet. A sick dizziness rolled over her, and she felt her knees dip. Luc's strong arms caught her, drawing her against his hard chest.

His eyes searched hers. "Do you need to sit down?"

She nodded. "I think so," she said as he guided her toward the overstuffed sofa in the sitting area at the front of her ranch cabin.

"Where's the kitchen? I'll get some water for you," he said.

"Straight down the hallway," she said, resting her head in her hands, castigating herself. If only she could have made Nicki listen! She'd repeatedly begged Nicki to get out of the fast lane, but Nicki had ignored her. Her younger sister had been determined to make a name for herself one way or another, and lately there'd been much more attention paid to Nicki's partying than to her acting abilities.

Luc returned with a glass of water and shook his head when she started to rise. "You're still pale," he said.

She took a sip of water and inhaled a shallow breath. "I should go to her."

"You can't," he said. "No one is allowed to see her during the detox phase."

She stared at him. "Not even a family member?"

"No one," he said. "It was a condition of getting her into this rehabilitation center. It has an excellent success rate."

Unable to sit any longer, Gwen rose to her feet. "I tried to get her to stop. I was able to persuade her to come out to the ranch for a few days. I hoped the fresh air and peace and just being away from the party scene would help. But her friends were always calling and sending her text messages. She got antsy and left early. I made her promise she would be more careful."

"She'll get the help she needs now."

Gwen fought the tears that filled her eyes. "I feel like such a failure. I should have—"

Luc put his hand over her shoulder. "She's an adult, free to make her own choices, right or wrong. You couldn't control her."

Intellectually, she knew he was right. She would have said the same thing to someone else in these circumstances, but it didn't stop the combination of guilt and helplessness gnawing at her.

Taking a deep breath, she felt a rush of gratitude for the Hudsons. They had gotten her sister to a safe place. "Thank you so much for taking care of her. I would have liked to have been the one to have been there for her, but at least she's getting help. It could have turned out so much worse."

He replied with a slow nod and gave her a long considering glance. "Everyone wants Nicki to get better. The problem is that this has happened at a critical time for Hudson Pictures. Nicki was supposed to be preparing to do promotion for *The Waiting Room*. Her stint in rehab could damage the way this movie is perceived by the press and the public."

Gwen remembered the PR routine from her years of acting. Although she'd left a promising acting career and Hollywood behind, she would have to have had amnesia to forget the promotional sprint required for movies—interviews with magazines, entertainment and news shows, public appearances.

"That is difficult," she acknowledged, then shrugged. "But with Nicki in rehab, there's really nothing that can be done."

Luc met her gaze with a resolution that made her uneasy. "I disagree," he said in a velvet voice with an underlay of steel. "In this case, the press needs a distraction. After taking care of Nicki last night, we held an emergency meeting and came up with a solution."

Gwen shrugged again, not sure why she needed to know this information. Her concern was Nicki, not Hudson Pictures. "I'm glad."

His lips rose in a crooked grin of irony. "We'll see." His amusement faded as quickly as a flash. "In order to keep the focus off Nicki, an announcement was made to the press last night. The announcement was that you and I are engaged."

Shock slammed through her. Gwen stared at him in disbelief. She blinked, shaking her head. She couldn't have heard him correctly. "Excuse me?"

"As far as the press is concerned, you and I are engaged to be married."

Gwen shook her head faster. "Oh, absolutely not. I don't even know you. I don't *want* to know you," she added to underscore her refusal. "Part of the reason I left Hollywood was to get away from the public relations racket that never stopped. No—"

"It's already done," he said in a firm voice. "If you don't want your sister's reputation to go down the toilet, then you'll cooperate."

The coolness in his voice dug at her. She took a second look into his eyes and glimpsed a ruthlessness that made her shudder. "This almost sounds like blackmail," she said.

"Call it what you want," he said. "I'm good, but I can't perform miracles. Your sister has made a huge mess, and someone's got to clean it up. Allowing *The Waiting Room* to tank because of her lack of maturity and discipline isn't going to help anyone, including her."

Gwen couldn't fight the urge to defend her sister. "You know nothing about the hurt Nicki has gone through. When my parents divorced it was at a very critical time for her, and she might as well have been orphaned for all the attention they gave her. She's been struggling with the damage ever since."

"That's what therapy is for," Luc said. "No one's life is perfect. At some point you have to grow up and take responsibility for who you are and what you want. Nicki is overdue."

Even if there was a bit of truth to his words, Gwen couldn't forgive his lack of compassion. "Easy for you to say that no one's life is perfect. I suspect yours has been pretty damn close. The perfect powerful Hudsons."

He shot her a wry smile. "The reason you think we're perfect and powerful is because I've done my job with the press. Just as I'm now doing my job for this movie and your sister."

Her sister was an afterthought, of course. His attitude infuriated her. "Nice try, but I can't believe it will work. I can't imagine that anyone would be interested in me anymore," she said. "I'm no longer in the Hollywood scene. As far as the paparazzi are concerned, I lead a quiet, boring life rescuing horses on my uncle's ranch. And that's they way I intend to keep it."

"Again, that's where you're wrong. You were a darling. Women wanted your combination of beauty and strength. Men just wanted you. Your last film came out a year ago, and when the DVD comes out in two weeks, it's projected to be a top seller."

Gwen swore under her breath. "So in PR terms, I'm one of the flavors of the moment," she said and felt the prospect of participating in Luc's scheme tighten around her like a straitjacket. "It still won't work. I have the ranch."

"The plan is for me to stay here at the ranch for a while. Then we'll make a big public splash in L.A. in a few weeks."

Her stomach turned. "I cannot fathom pretending to be your adoring fiancée for three seconds."

"You won a Golden Globe and were nominated for an Oscar. This will be cake."

"Cake," she echoed in disbelief. "I might as well be engaged to the devil. I was married to a man who only wanted me for—" She broke off. The memory of all that had taken place between her and her husband was still too painful. "I can't pretend that way again."

"You can for your sister," he countered.

Gwen stomped to the front closet and grabbed her boots. She felt so trapped, so impotent that she could scream. This would be a fine time to muck out the stalls. Heaven knew, she needed to work off some of her extra energy threatening to erupt any second. She kicked off her shoes and shoved her feet into the boots, trying to ignore the tall, imposing figure of Luc Hudson standing three feet away from her.

"Where do you want me to stay while I'm here? You have a guest room?"

A few searing, scathing responses kicked through her brain about exactly where she would like Luc to go, but she bit the inside of her cheek to keep from saying them.

He gave a wry chuckle. "I realize you'd prefer I stay in the barn," he said.

"Oh, no. I wouldn't want to punish the horses," she said. "Go down the hallway and take the second door on the right. It has a brass bed and a sheepskin rug on the floor beside it. You can have that room," she said and left the house with a small sense of satisfaction. Although putting Luc in that bedroom meant he would be sleeping next door to her, entirely too close for her comfort, she loved the idea that he would be living in a pink room for the time he was here. She'd decorated the room with Nicki in mind, so the walls were pink, the balloon shades fashioned from a French floral sateen of pink and blue that matched the floral quilt on the bed. A lace bedskirt coordinated with lace pillows on the bed and a cozy pastel blue upholstered rocker sat beside the bed.

All that pink would drive Luc, a man dripping with masculinity, out of his mind. And if she were lucky, out of her house and life.

Luc carried his suitcase into his assigned room and surveyed his new digs. He wiped his hand over his eyes and face. The girly room was a far cry from the clean, cool lines of his contemporary home decorated in black and white. Glancing at the puffy window treatments, he felt his skin begin to itch as if he were having an allergic reaction.

How was he supposed to get any work done in this room? The dresser was covered with girly knickknacks. Luc couldn't stand clutter. His job was to fix the clutter and chaos that other people created. That was the reason he was here.

His mind wandered to the woman who would help him carry off the charade. She was even more potent in person than she'd been onscreen. With each change of emotion, her expressive eyes and face grabbed and held his attention. Luc was good at reading people within the first thirty seconds of a personal meeting, but Gwen was too complex.

It hadn't been necessary to read her dossier. Her history had been splashed on every magazine and newspaper. Rumors had swirled that her affair with a costar had caused the demise of her high-profile marriage to one of Hollywood's top producers. Then she'd disappeared.

Her beauty and talent obviously had not disappeared. Neither had the simmering sensuality that boiled beneath her composed surface. If Luc hadn't learned his lesson about getting involved with actresses, he would be tempted to learn Gwen's secrets in and out of bed, but he knew better.

His cell phone rang, and he immediately identified the ring that belonged to his brother Max. "Hey, I made it."

"I decided I should check, since I hadn't heard from you."

"It took me longer than I expected to rent the SUV. Gwen's ranch is dead center in the middle of nowhere. You can tell she wanted to leave the 'City of Angels' far behind."

"How did she respond to the news?"

"Depends on which news," Luc said, moving closer to the window and studying how to disconnect the curtains. "She was upset about Nicki, wanted to go see her."

"You nixed that," his brother said.

"Yeah."

"And how did the lovely lady feel about your impending nuptials?" his brother cracked.

Luc frowned and shook his head. "The things I do for the family business. Let's just put it this way—I'm glad she didn't have any sharp instruments close by when I told her."

Max gave a low chuckle. "You mean she wasn't dying to get involved with one of the town's most sought-after bachelors?"

"You're having a little too much fun with this."

"Maybe you could have some fun too if you play your cards right. Gwen McCord was damn hot. Didn't she make the sexiest females list of some magazine years ago?"

Several magazines. Luc recalled one particularly memorable shot of her from one of her movies where she was dressed in a man's unbuttoned shirt and nothing else. The photograph had exposed a generous amount of creamy cleavage, hinted at dusky nipples beneath and revealed shapely legs that went on forever. The tip of her tongue touching her upper lip and long bangs covering one of her eyes was the stuff to fuel the fantasies of millions of men young and old. Luc pushed the arousing image from his mind. "The only way Gwen is hot right now is how furious she is with me and the Hudsons."

"Oh, she's lost her looks already?"

"No," Luc said in exasperation. "She's still beautiful, but she's angry that she's been forced into this engagement."

"She ought to be grateful we got her crazy sister in rehab so quickly," Max said.

"She is. She just doesn't want to be dragged into the public eye again." Opening the closet door, he found it mostly empty. Relief oozed through him. Thank God. He could stuff the knickknacks and lacy crap in there.

"You think she'll go along with it?" his brother asked.

"She doesn't have a choice. That's why she's so pissed," Luc said. "Her frustration isn't important as long as she cooperates."

"I've heard that take-no-prisoners tone from you

before," Max said. "I don't know whether to feel sorry for you or her."

"I don't need any pity," Luc said, glancing at the pink walls and grinding his teeth. "I can take care of myself."

After Gwen mucked out the stalls and fed the horses, she returned to the house, still bothered, but under control. She temporarily left her boots at the front door and made her way toward her bedroom. The smell of something delicious wafted from the kitchen. The door to the room where Luc Hudson would be sleeping was open. When she glanced inside, she nearly got whiplash.

Luc sat in the blue chair working on his laptop, but the curtains were gone, along with all the pillows, the collection of figurines and porcelain jewelry boxes and every picture on the wall. A dark comforter she suspected he'd found in the hall linen closet covered the bed. The windows were bare.

She stepped inside. "Where are—"

"In the closet," he said before she could finish. He stood. "I did some temporary redecorating. I'll put it all back before I leave. Although the furnishings were—" he paused a half beat "—lovely, they were distracting. I have to be able to concentrate on my work."

She glanced at the bare windows and nodded. "Okay," she said. He would be waking up at the crack of dawn, but that wasn't her problem. "No problem. What do I sme—"

"My chef prepared a couple of meals before I left," Luc said. "When I told her I was leaving for Montana, she was convinced I was going to be stuck in the wilderness in a blizzard." He glanced outside the window at the falling snow. "She was half-right. Are you hungry?"

Her instinct was to say no. After all, she didn't want him here. He was uninvited and he was interrupting the peaceful world she'd worked so hard to build for herself. Her stomach rumbled silently, and Gwen decided it didn't have to mean anything if she ate some of his food. Otherwise she would be facing her own cooking, which left a lot to be desired.

"A little," she conceded.

"You're welcome to it," he said. "Roast chicken and some vegetables. And homemade bread," he added in a warning tone. "No woman in L.A. will touch bread."

Homemade bread. Gwen tried to conceal her excitement as her feet moved of their own accord to the kitchen. "I'm not in L.A.," she said, hearing him follow her. She saw a box with handles on the counter. "They let you bring that on the plane?" she asked.

"I chartered a jet," he said.

"Oh, right," Gwen said, remembering the occasional times when she'd also flown on a chartered flight. Those days were over since she'd left her film career behind. She rarely regretted the loss of the perks from her glamorous career. One exception was the service of a chef. Cooking had never been her forte.

She glanced inside the box and inhaled the scent of fresh bread. Heaven. She reluctantly met Luc's gaze. "You're sure you don't mind sharing?"

"Not at all," he said, amusement tugging at his sensual mouth. "I would have never dreamed you'd be so enthusiastic about carbs."

She shouldn't like him. He was powerful, oozed confidence and probably always got his way. She couldn't help smiling in commiseration. "One of the top-ten wonderful things about leaving Hollywood is being able to indulge myself with forbidden foods more often. Thank you," she said and took a bite of the fresh bread.

He pulled some containers from the refrigerator. "I noticed your refrigerator's bare except for frozen dinners. Where's your staff?"

"My uncle, who owns the ranch, offered to share his housekeeper with me, but I don't want to cause any extra expense during the transition phase," she said and put the food on a plate, then placed it into the microwave.

"So my chef wasn't far off the mark," he said, resting his hands on his hips.

"My focus right now is getting up to speed on managing the rescue operations of the ranch. I eventually want to add a summer camp for disadvantaged children. Cooking for myself isn't a big priority. If you're concerned about food, you can always stay in town. There's a diner and fast-food restaurant, a motel and—"

He shook his head. "You and I have to be together in order to sell the story."

The microwave alarm dinged and Gwen removed the food. Her mouth watered in anticipation. Just as she pulled a knife and fork from a drawer, her cell phone rang. Glancing at the Caller ID, she immediately picked up. "Hello?"

"Gwen, this is Robert Williams with the fire department. We have a report of a mare stuck in an icy pond on the McAllister property. If we can get her out alive, do you want to rescue her?"

The image of the trapped horse flashed through her mind, and her heart tightened. "She doesn't belong to any of the ranchers who live close by?"

"No. They're pretty sure she's wild."

"Wow," Gwen said, adrenaline rushing through her veins. "Yes. I'll call Dennis and the vet and bring over the trailer. Thanks." She pushed the off button and speed-dialed Dennis, the operations manager for the entire ranch, but it went straight to voice mail. "Darn," she muttered, remembering that Dennis had taken his wife into town to celebrate their anniversary. He'd probably turned off his cell.

"What's wrong?" Luc asked.

"I need to go pick up a horse for rescue. Dennis usually goes with me."

"I can help you," he said.

She shot him a look of disbelief. "This is a wild horse. If the fire department can get her out of the freezing pond, she still may not be cooperative."

"A close friend of my parents owns a ranch. I spent summers there when I was a kid and teenager. I worked with the trainer when he broke a couple wild ponies."

"Really?" she said, surprised. As one of the privileged Hudsons, Luc struck her as the kind of man who would demand and receive only the best and most cutting-edge conveniences in his life. She would have bet money that the only physical challenges he faced were conducted in a temperature-controlled gym...or perhaps the bedroom. She immediately pushed that thought aside. Where had it come from anyway?

"Yes, really. Shouldn't we be going?" he asked. "I'll grab my coat, hat and gloves."

Rattled by the intensity in his expression, she nodded. Without Dennis around, she would be a fool to reject Luc's offer of assistance. "Okay," she said and pulled out plastic wrap to cover the food and put it in the refrigerator.

"Bring that plate with you?" he asked over his shoulder as he walked toward the room where he was staying.

"I can't eat and drive," she called after him, but he didn't appear to be listening.

Less than a minute later, he appeared in the hallway dressed for the outdoors. "I'll drive. You can navigate in between bites."

"That truck has a stick shift and an ornery clutch."

"I can handle it," he said with a level gaze that let her know he could handle a lot more than she'd suspected he could. He moved his athletic body with a sensual confidence that went deeper than skin, leaving no doubt that he could take care of a woman in every possible way.

Looking at him reminded her that it had been eons since she'd been held by a man, even longer since she'd made love. She'd told herself she didn't miss having a man in her life. She didn't miss having someone take her breath away with just a look, someone who could make her heart stop and start just by saying her name. She sure as heck didn't miss the pain that followed when she made herself vulnerable.

She suspected he was a master seducer and lover, the kind of man to leave a woman begging for more. Gwen resolved not to be that woman.

Two

Within minutes of when Gwen and Luc had arrived at the rescue site, Gwen knew she'd underestimated Luc Hudson. Standing at the edge of the pond with freezing water rising to the tops of his boots, he used a chainsaw to break up the ice that covered most of the pond.

Gwen's apprehension rose with each passing second. As soon as the chill overtook the mare, the horse would lose a lot of her fight and the job of rescuing her would grow more difficult than ever. Colored chestnut-brown, with a white star on her forehead, the horse was drenched, her eyes wide with fear and distress. She wanted out, but she was afraid of the men.

The men looped a rope over the mare's head. She

fought the rope for a couple of minutes. Since she was wild, she didn't understand that they were trying to help her. Luc helped spread a tarp over the ice he had pulverized.

When one of the men waded into the water wearing an orange suit and carrying another rope for the horse's hindquarters, Gwen rushed to grab one of the ropes from the shore.

Luc shook his head. "You don't need to be out here. Get the trailer ready."

"The trailer's ready," she retorted.

"He has a point," said Dan, the fireman holding the rope next to her. "This is a job for someone with more upper-body strength."

Frustration twisted inside her, and she passed the rope to one of the other firemen. "I'll back the trailer a few feet closer."

"Good idea," Dan said. "We're going to need to get her inside as soon as possible."

The wind sliced like a vicious whip, and sleet pelted her down jacket like tiny needles of ice. Gwen climbed into the truck and started the engine, then backed up a few feet until she heard one of the men yell. She exited the truck and checked the trailer again.

Luc waved for her to come to him. "Here," he said, taking a digital camera from his pocket.

"What?" she asked in dismay. "You want me to take pictures?"

"No, I want you to shoot video," he said. "Stand over there," he said. "The light will be better."

"Have you lost your mind?"

"No," he said. "Trust me. You'll thank me later. Shoot the video. Press this button when I tell you to start."

"This is ridiculous. I need to be helping that horse the second she gets out of the pond."

"We're going to take her straight into the trailer. There's nothing else you can do. This will be great PR for your cause."

She tasted the bitter flavor of cynicism in the back of her throat. "PR," she said in disgust. "I should have known. You have a one-track mind."

His eyes turned cold as the ice surrounding them. "PR is what will bring in the donations you need if you're going to continue to rescue these horses." He shrugged. "Don't say I didn't warn you."

"Hoo," the man in the water called. "She's on the move. This could be it."

Conflicted by Luc's comments, Gwen stepped aside, watching the mare thrash toward shore.

"Now," Luc called and Gwen pushed the button for recording video. With her heart pounding at the mare's distress, it took everything inside her to focus on the drama unfolding before her.

The mare stumbled and the men struggled to get her back on her feet. Her mouth dipped into the freezing water, and Gwen's heart stopped.

Luc gently tugged the rope and spoke to the mare in a deep coaxing voice. "C'mon, baby, you can do it. Just a little more. We're gonna take care of you."

The mare dipped her mouth into the water again, then lifted it and shook her head. With a surge of energy and a synergy that was nearly mystical, the horse moved forward, Luc pulled and the fireman in the water pushed.

The mare stumbled up the tarp onto land, and Luc and the others immediately led her into the trailer. "You can stop now," he yelled to Gwen.

Gwen blinked, automatically following his command. She'd been so tense she could barely move. She forced her feet to move toward the trailer. Luc snapped the back of the trailer closed and looked up at her.

His gaze met hers, and she felt a click that reverberated all the way down to her feet. In that instant, she understood what Luc Hudson was about. He would go to the wall for what he considered important. As far as the press was concerned, he would play them like a concert pianist to produce exactly the music he wanted. Power and passion emanated from him.

She fought a breathtaking combination of attraction and terror. Gwen realized she'd never met a man quite like him before.

"Ready?" he said.

Gwen nodded, hoping her strange feelings were like lightning, here for one second and gone the next.

Luc pulled the truck to a stop outside a large barn. Two men rushed outside to greet them.

"Good," Gwen murmured and glanced at him. "The vet and ranch manager."

Nodding, Luc got out of the car. Gwen exited from her side at the same time. "Carl, Dennis, this is Luc Hudson. He's visiting and he helped with the rescue."

Luc extended his hand to the two men. "I hope you have access to some warmers," he said.

"Already set up," Carl said. "I talked to the fire department while you two were in transit. They said you were a big help."

"Glad to pitch in," he said.

"I'm sorry to interrupt your anniversary," Gwen said to Dennis.

The ruddy-faced man smiled and nodded. "Hey, at least we got a meal out." He winked. "More if I get back early enough." A thump sounded from the trailer. "This one sounds impatient. We'd better get her inside."

It required quite a bit of coaxing and maneuvering, but the four of them managed to get the mare into a large stall. She didn't appear happy with her confinement, but she readily drank the water available for her.

The more Luc studied the horse, the more suspicious he became. He glanced at Gwen, and she looked up at him at the same moment.

"She's pregnant," they both said at the same time.

Gwen gave a breathless laugh and blinked, meeting his gaze as if she was curious about him but didn't want to be.

Her expression made something in his gut tie into a knot. She reminded him a bit of the mare—strong, with a wild streak, but skittish as the day was long.

She looked away. "Carl, do you think the baby will be okay?"

"Give me time to examine her," the vet said, nudging his shoulder against the horse and talking softly to her.

Luc watched Gwen cross her arms over her chest and bite her lush lip. She was a complex woman, different from any he'd met lately, if ever. When she'd been in the Hollywood scene, her hair color had been a brighter blonde and she'd always looked cool and polished.

Luc liked her current look better. With honey-colored hair, a face scrubbed free of cosmetics and fingernails without polish, she looked warmer, more real. More touchable.

In another circumstance, he would wonder if her curly dark eyelashes were false and if the bright color of her green eyes came courtesy of tinted contact lenses, but he knew better. She was one of the rare actresses whose beauty easily conquered the unforgiving scrutiny of Hi-Def.

Watching her fidget, he moved closer. "What are you going to name her?"

She glanced up at him with a blank expression. "I have no idea."

"She's strong. I'd bet on her survival."

"You would?" she asked, her gaze straying to the mare.

"Sure. Wouldn't you?"

She looked at him and slowly nodded. "Thank you for helping. I didn't expect—"

He lifted his hand to cut her off. "My pleasure. Really."

She narrowed her eyes and studied him for a moment. "I can't quite figure you out. One minute, I'm sure your defining character quality is operating the PR machine. The next minute…"

He raised his eyebrows. "The next minute?" he prompted.

"The next minute you're insisting I eat your food or helping to rescue a horse."

"Trust your first instinct," he couldn't resist saying in a dry tone. "I'm completely one-dimensional. A cynical, heartless prick."

She blinked, surprise widening her eyes for a full moment before she did a double take. Then she shook her head and laughed. "Okay, thanks for the warning."

"I think she's gonna be okay," the vet called from inside the stall. "You're going to have a tougher time with her when she gets the rest of her strength back, which will be soon, so be prepared."

Gwen walked closer to the stall. "What about those scrapes from the ice?"

"She didn't like my cleaning them, but I did it anyway. I was able to give her an antibiotic without her killing me. Her temperature's close to normal, so that's good."

"What about the baby?"

The vet nodded. "So far, so good. Keep the monitor on tonight, and I'll drop by tomorrow."

"Thanks for coming out," Dennis said. "If it's okay with you, I'm going to head back to my wife. Call my cell if you need me. Otherwise, I'll be here first thing in the morning."

"You go on home. I'll stay here for a while," Gwen said.

"Okay, g'night," Dennis said, tipping his head. "Thanks for your help, Luc."

"You're welcome," Luc said.

The two men left and Gwen turned to Luc. "You can go back to the house now. I'll be okay."

Luc shrugged. "I'll stay."

"It's really not necessary," she said. "I don't need—"

"You never know," he said. "I came in handy before."

She gave a reluctant nod. "Okay," she said and went to the tack room. Luc wandered around the barn, looking at the horses in their stalls and taking in the layout. Inhaling the scents of hay and horseflesh, he was taken back to the summers he'd spent at his father's friend's ranch. Not many people knew it, but there'd been a time when Luc had secretly considered becoming a rancher. Before he'd graduated from high school, though, it had become clear that Hudson Pictures would need him.

He moved back to the stall belonging to the pregnant mare and watched Gwen hang a bridle just inside the mare's stall.

"Good move," he said. "You want her to get used to the idea of the bridle, so you put it where she can see it and smell it."

"One of the many things my uncle and Dennis have taught me. Look at how tired she is," Gwen said in a soft voice. "Her head's drooping."

"She's fighting sleep. It could be days before she really rests. Horses won't truly rest unless they feel safe, but it's probably best for her lungs for her to wait awhile anyway."

She glanced at him in surprise. "That's more than passing knowledge about horses."

"I told you I spent several summers on the ranch of a family friend."

She studied him for a moment. Her curiosity emanated from her like air from a fan. "You're a Hudson. You've got the connections and the background. Why didn't you go into acting?"

He laughed. "Not my forte and never my secret desire. I'm great in front of the media for fifteen minutes, thirty minutes max."

"Then what?"

"The real me comes out," he said.

Her lips curved upward in humor. "How scary is that?"

"Pretty damn scary," he said.

"Then why did you choose PR?"

"More of a case of it choosing me. Hudson Pictures is bigger than me. I may have played with the idea of doing something else, but I always knew I would be a part of it. Family, heritage, destiny," he added in a mock melodramatic tone.

"That's the way I feel about this ranch. About rescuing horses. It's bigger than me."

"Making movies wasn't?" he asked.

"This is real," she said. "Movies are make-believe."

He stepped closer to her. "But you have to admit that pictures serve a purpose. They make people laugh when they're depressed. They entertain and educate."

"True, but I'm more at peace now than I've ever been in my entire life."

"Some would call it hiding."

She tossed her head. "Some can call it whatever they want. It's most important what *I* call it." She shot him a sideways glance. "Are you sure you don't want to go back to the house?"

He laughed at her obvious effort to get rid of him. "I would have thought you were a woman who likes a challenge."

"Depends whether the challenge is worth my time,"

she said in a cool voice as she met his gaze again. Her voice might be cool, but her eyes were hot.

The combination was seductive for Luc. A forbidden image of Gwen, naked and hot in his bed, sliced through his brain. The woman made him curious. He took another tack and nodded toward the mare. "How's the mom-to-be looking?"

She turned her attention to the horse and sighed. "Resting as well as she can," she said, weariness creeping into her tone.

"You sound tired. You've had a rough day. Why don't *you* go back to the house?"

She wrapped her arms around herself. "I'll fall asleep as soon as I get there and I should stay awake."

"Don't you have cameras you can watch from the house?"

"Yes, but—"

"I could watch while you rest," he said.

"Why would you do that?"

"I'm not as tired as you are. Besides," he said, shooting her a wicked grin, "what kind of man would I be if I didn't look after my fiancée?"

She rolled her eyes. "Oh, don't remind me. I'd almost forgotten about that."

"You'll get reminders soon enough. I wouldn't be surprised if the paparazzi didn't show up on your doorstep."

"It wouldn't be the first time," she said. "I just usually try to bore them with politeness before I tell them I don't give interviews anymore."

"That's a mistake," he said. "At some point, you're going to need financial support in order to maintain your rescue operation. You could get a lot of mileage out of your film background."

"I'm not interested in that kind of mileage," she said as she took a seat in the chair opposite the mare's stall. "You can still leave…"

"No. Someone needs to catch you when you fall off that chair," he said, leaning against the wall.

She raised her chin in mute protest but didn't engage him further.

Surprisingly enough, the silence was peaceful instead of hostile. The moments passed and Luc drank in the quiet, wondering how long it had been since he'd experienced such a lack of sound. Either his cell was ringing or he was creating the next spin or taking care of the latest crisis.

He drew in a deep breath of the cool air. Hmm. Maybe Gwen had a point. As busy as he'd been today, the atmosphere at the ranch made him feel less cluttered, more calm. Glancing at her to make a comment, he stopped before he swallowed a chuckle at the sight of her with her head rolled back against the wall and her eyes closed, her breath slow and even.

Watching her for the next few moments, he didn't make a move until her head began to slide downward. He caught her shoulders just as her eyes fluttered open, but he held her right where she was.

She blinked. "What are you doing?"

His gut tightened like a vise. He inhaled her sexy, spicy scent, so at odds with the earthy smell of the barn. Her skin bare of makeup looked as smooth as satin with the slightest bloom of pink in her cheeks. And her mouth, Lord help him. Lush puffy lips the color of roses would haunt his dreams for nights.

"What are you doing?" she repeated, her voice husky.

"Catching you," he said, flexing his hands. "Catching you before you fall."

Three

Gwen's breath stopped in her chest. Excitement whipped through her, shocking her with its intensity. She shook her head and deliberately pushed Luc away. "I'm not falling," she said and stood, irritated that she felt a little wobbly. "I'm fine," she said, determined to be exactly that.

Watching her, he slowly rose and nodded. "Good."

Hating that he seemed to be able to see beneath her skin, she walked to the stall and watched the mare for a few moments. Feeling Luc's presence just behind her, Gwen glanced at her watch. She would need to rise early in the morning. "I'm going back to the house. Tomorrow will be a busy day."

"I'll go with you," he said and walked beside her as she closed up the barn.

During the last two years, Gwen had spent a lot of time by herself, and that time had been good for her. She'd had the chance to mourn her losses in private. Every once in a while, she'd wished for human companionship but not enough to do anything about it. As for romantic relationships, by the time her divorce from Peter had been final, she'd felt as cold as a frozen lake, and there'd been no thawing.

Snow and sleet pelted her head and shoulders.

"Wicked weather," Luc said. "How does a California girl stand the cold?"

"I'm not a California girl anymore. I love the snow. There's nothing like that peaceful quiet after a freshly fallen snow. It's almost as if the acoustics of the earth change for that bit of time."

He nodded. "I never thought of it that way, but I guess they do," he said. "The same way they change during a thunderstorm, or an earthquake. Do you feel the same way about sleet and ice?"

"It's more dangerous," she admitted. "But I'm lucky. My uncle installed backup generators for my cabin and the rescue barns."

"And you don't ever miss the ocean or warm weather," he said, his voice full of disbelief. "Especially during winter."

She pursed her lips together, wanting to refute him, but knowing it was a lie. "Every now and then, I miss the warmth. It's a trade-off." She chuckled to herself. "Plus it keeps the paparazzi away. Only a desperate fool is going to show up in this kind of weather to get a photograph of a has-been actress."

"Has-been," he echoed, stopping in front of her so that she also was forced to stop. His expression was incredulous. "Is that the way you see yourself? Because you could damn well name your price and part if—"

She shook her head and smiled. "I'm a happy has-been." His intense gaze seemed to delve inside her as if he could glimpse her secrets. Uneasy, she stepped to the side to move around him, but her foot hit an icy patch and she began to slide. "Damn—"

He caught her and pulled her against his hard chest, making her instantly aware of his strength, stealing her breath away again. She bit her lip. "I'm okay. I don't need—"

"Maybe not, but I was raised to try to prevent women from falling on the ground. That's three times today."

His eyes were full of curiosity and a too-appealing blend of humor and irony. She felt a pop of her own curiosity. A reluctant knight. Who would have thought it? What other secrets lay beneath the Hudson PR exterior?

She pushed away from him. "I'll tell you a secret. No one's looking. You could have let me fall on my—*self*, and no one would have noticed."

He shrugged. "I would have. Besides, you've had a rough day. Your sister, your engagement to me, the horse."

"You can fix one of those," she said, growing increasingly uncomfortable with his invasion of her little universe.

"Which one?"

"The engagement. You could make it go away. *You* could go away."

He chuckled. "No chance. We're both stuck for the duration. If you don't like it, just think of it the same

way you do the weather. It's a trade-off." He rested his
hands on his hips. "So go on to the cabin before I'm
struck with a sudden obligation to carry you."

"God forbid," Gwen muttered and trudged forward.
She would nap in the office tonight so she could watch
the monitors of the rescue barn. Every step she took, she
heard the crunch of Luc's boots just behind hers. She
heard his breath. Right there behind her, watching her,
he was waiting to catch her if necessary. The notion
made her stomach turn a flip, a sensation she hadn't experienced in years. She didn't like it.

Hours later, she awakened to the sound of a knock at
the front door. She sat up in bed, confused, realizing she
was still dressed in the same jeans and flannel shirt she'd
worn the day before. *What? How?* She brushed her hair
from her eyes, trying to blink away her drowsiness.

Mentally backtracking, she recalled coming into the
cabin and settling into the office so she could steal a few
naps in between watching the mare from the remote
camera feed. How had she ended up in her bed?

Another knock sounded at the door. She heard a low
male voice. Luc Hudson, she remembered and pushed
her quilt aside. She glanced at the clock and cringed.
Seven a.m. She should have been up by five! Dashing
to the bathroom, she splashed water on her face and
brushed her teeth, then rushed down the hall. She took
a turn toward the office.

"Gwen, dear," Luc called.

She stopped midstep, frowning at the *dear*. She
swung around to look at him. He stood in the doorway

backlit and looking wide-eyed and perfectly awake. She tried not to snarl.

A man she'd never seen before craned around him and lifted a camera, taking a half-dozen shots as she stared in surprise. Luc shoved the door closed and strode toward her.

"They're already here," he said.

"Who?" she asked, craving a cup or ten of coffee. "And how did I end up—"

"We don't have time. We'll have to talk later." He ran his fingers through her hair. "Put this on," he said, pulling a jeweler's box from his pocket and opening it. Lifting the large solitaire with a diamond-studded band, he caught her left hand and pushed the ring onto her finger.

Gwen gaped at the ring, shocked at how well it fit. "How did you know—"

"Pretend you're madly in love with me," he said and tugged her toward the front door.

"But what—"

"The paparazzi," he said and opened the door.

Gwen immediately heard a dozen clicks from the camera. "When did you and Luc Hudson get involved?" another man asked. "And what's going on with your sister, Nicki?"

Luc slid his arm around her waist. "Gotta give you guys credit. You're the first. You make it damn hard to keep a relationship private." He turned toward Gwen and dipped his head. "I think they've caught us, sweet-heart," he said and lowered his mouth to hers.

Gwen blinked in surprise at the sensation of his lips on hers. Hearing the click of the camera reminded her of her role, Luc's adoring fiancée. She deliberately melted against him and lifted her hand to his bicep. His kiss felt both foreign and natural. His body was warm and strong, his hand at her back firm and persuasive. His mouth lingered, catching her off guard, but she recovered, ducking her head into his shoulder.

"So shy. Listen, why don't you come back later? We can show you the horse we rescued yesterday. She's pregnant."

"Gwen's pregnant?" the reporter asked.

Gwen felt as if she'd been slapped. "No," she said immediately in a sharp voice. "*The horse* is pregnant. Not me."

"Okay," the reporter said, sounding disappointed. "Let me get a shot of the rock. Everyone likes to see the ring."

Gwen raised her hand and stared at the unfamiliar ring on her finger.

"Cool, you look like you can't believe it," the reporter said.

The man had no idea, Gwen thought and plastered a pleasant expression on her face.

He glanced at Luc. "You'll let us shoot some film?"

"It'll make you understand even more why I fell for her."

The photographer glanced at Gwen. "As if you needed a reason," he said. "Hollywood misses you, Gwen."

Gwen smiled, amused by how glamorous she didn't look with zero makeup, hair that hadn't been brushed and sleepy eyes. Good thing she didn't give a rip. "You're too kind." She wrapped her hand around Luc's bicep. "There's a diner in town if you're hungry."

"Okay," the reporter said. "You promise you won't go anywhere?"

"We're not going anywhere," Luc assured the man.

The reporter nodded. "This is gonna be great. So, I'm Tripp and this is Gordon." Both men exchanged handshakes with her and Luc. "See you in an hour."

"Two would be better," Luc said.

"Okay," Tripp said reluctantly. "Two hours, but not one minute more."

The two men ran to their car and exchanged a high five before getting in and leaving. Disgusted, Gwen shut the front door and immediately rounded on Luc. "Why did you invite the paparazzi to hang around and shoot film? I don't want them on the ranch."

"They won't be here that long," he said. "This is perfect. They won't be focusing their full attention on us."

"I don't want this ranch exploited for the almighty sake of Hudson Pictures. This is a beautiful, peaceful, safe place for the horses and—"

"And for you," Luc interjected. "A safe place for you to hide from the rest of the world."

Something inside her twisted. His words were like a hot poker fresh from the fire, stabbing at her most vulnerable point. "You have no right to criticize the life I've chosen. You have no right to invite these—" she broke off, her frustration growing by the millisecond "—these parasites onto my uncle's property just because it serves your purpose. After years of working non-stop, my uncle is finally taking that three-week cruise he deserves. I hate to see his reaction when he returns to this mess. Have you thought about what will happen after this? How many more reporters will show up once our photos hit the rag sheets? And after this charade is over, how am I supposed to handle the reporters who keep showing up, asking for an explanation of why you and I broke up?"

Luc met her gaze with infuriating calm. "You can trust me. I'll handle this."

She rolled her eyes. "I've heard that before. *Trust me* are the two most deadly words in Hollywood."

"Like you said yesterday, we're not in Hollywood. I've been handling the press for years, Gwen. I can handle them this time, too. If it gets too intense, I'll bring in some security."

"Great," she said, her voice full of sarcasm. "Exactly what I wanted. Security."

"It's temporary. And you shouldn't knock the publicity you'll get. You'll get a flood of donations for horse rescue after this airs."

She sighed, hating that he was right. "I need to get a shower. I don't know how I ended up in my bed with my clothes still on. Last thing I remembered I was in my office watching the mare on the monitor and—" She stopped, seeing the knowing expression on his face. "Oh, don't tell me you carried me to bed."

"I did it for myself. Your head was cradled in your hands. You were going to end up with a helluva neck ache. You're already difficult enough without anything else added."

She opened her mouth to retort but couldn't think of a suitable response. Was she supposed to thank him for his thoughtfulness or rip him to shreds for daring to touch her while she was asleep? She wasn't accustomed to having anyone watch over her, especially a man such as Luc Hudson.

"I need to know how long this is going to last," she said. "And don't tell me 'however long it takes.' You know better. I bet you have this planned down to the minute. How long?"

"Barring complications with your sister, thirty to forty-five days," he said.

Gwen told herself it was just another shoot. Her last shoot.

Two hours later, Luc watched Gwen engage both the reporter and the photographer as she showed them the rescued pregnant horse. "She's still skittish and afraid, so you'll need to keep your distance. Isn't she a beauty?"

Tripp, the reporter, nodded. "She is. Did you know she was pregnant when you rescued her?"

Gwen shook her head. "We didn't find out until we moved her back to the ranch. Luc stepped right up and helped the firemen with the rescue."

"Really?" the reporter said, looking at Luc. "Never knew you were a horse lover."

"You never asked," Luc said in a deliberately cryptic voice and slid his arm around Gwen's waist.

Tripp gave a knowing nod. "Trying to impress your lady."

"It worked," Gwen said, playing her role well. "But I was impressed before."

"How did the two of you get involved?"

"We met at an industry function years ago and

were reintroduced when Gwen made a trip to L.A. a few months ago. I wasn't going to let her get away this time."

"The commute is rough, though. How do you handle it?"

"I have access to a jet. I can get here just about anytime I want."

"Any chance you'll lure her back into the movies?" Gordon asked.

Luc immediately felt Gwen stiffen. "I'm a lot more interested in luring her down the aisle."

"Have you set a date for the big day?" Tripp asked.

"We just got engaged," Gwen chided, nestling against Luc and looking up at him with such adoration he could understand every one of her nominations. The woman was damn convincing. "We've waited a long time to find each other, and we want to enjoy every minute." She paused a half beat. "Speaking of minutes, I have that appointment in town this afternoon," she said. "So, you'll have to excuse us. I really need to be going."

The photographer began to click photographs at a machine-gun speed. Gwen rose on tiptoe and skimmed her lush lips over his cheek then slid her mouth next to his ear. "Please get rid of them," she whispered, then nuzzled him again.

"That will be all," he said to the reporter and photographer. "Gwen and I have other things we need to do." He slid his hand down Gwen's arm to catch her hand. "I know you appreciate getting this exclusive scoop."

"More than you know, man. More than you know," Tripp said and extended his hand. "Thanks for working with us. You won't be sorry. And good luck with the horse, Gwen. What are you going to name her?"

"I hadn't—"

"Pyrrha," Luc said, looking at Gwen as she whipped around to meet his gaze.

"Pyrrha?" she echoed.

"Greek mythology. She was a queen."

"A survivor of the great flood," she said, her lips curving in a slow but genuine smile as she nodded. He felt a sizzle of connection resonate between them. "I like that."

Luc heard the rapid-fire click of the camera and felt a surge of annoyance. The media had worn out their welcome. He shook hands with Tripp. "Have a safe trip back to L.A.," he said and ushered everyone outdoors. He walked Gwen to the cabin.

"Did you manufacture the appointment to get rid of the reporters, or is it real?" he asked.

"It's real," she said over her shoulder as she climbed the stairs. "But I was ready for them to leave. In fact, it would have been fine with me if they'd never shown up in the first place."

"You'll be glad when you see the donations pouring in for your rescue operation," he said, wishing he could get a look at her long, lean legs without the benefit of denim covering them.

He closed the door behind them, and she turned to face him. "Why do you care about my rescue operation?"

He shrugged. "It's a good cause. If you and I are forced into this little charade, you may as well benefit from it."

She sighed, her eyes full of misgivings. "I just wonder

how many donors will be asking for their money back after our so-called engagement is over."

"We don't have to give the engagement a dramatic ending. Unlike your—" He broke off when he saw her gaze turn chilly.

"Comments like that are exactly why I hate dealing with the press. If they can't twist it to suit their purposes, they'll make something up. Trust me, you know nothing about the reason my marriage broke up." She glanced at her watch. "I need to go. I don't want to be late for the kids."

"Kids," he echoed.

She raised her hand. "None of your business. You've exploited me enough."

Her accusation jabbed him. He shot out his hand to catch her arm and pulled her back toward him. "Have you forgotten why we're doing this in the first place?"

She took a deep breath and bit her lip. "Nicki."

"Yes, Nicki. Do you want the press to crucify her?"

She closed her eyes and shook her head. "No. The more I think about it, the more I agree with you. I just find the whole paparazzi thing vile."

"So, it's not personal," he said in a wry voice.

"No," she said. "It's not personal. You're actually—" She broke off and shrugged. "Maybe we should start over. Hi, I'm Gwen McCord. It's nice to meet you."

He closed his hand over hers. "My pleasure," he said, playing along. "I'm Luc Hudson. You're even more enchanting in person than on the big screen."

She smiled. "Thank you. You're more helpful than I would have expected one of the Hudsons to be. I realize neither of us is thrilled with our assignment, but starting now I'll try not to make it more difficult than it already is. Who knows? By the end of this, we may even be friends."

Nodding, he lifted her hand to his lips, seeing in her eyes a spark of surprise mixed with something else. "To friendship," he said, but at that moment he decided they would be more than friends.

Four

Whenever Gwen returned from working with the after-school program in drama therapy, she struggled with a clashing sense of satisfaction and grief. If things had turned out differently, her own child would be in preschool now. Peter had demanded, however, that she finish filming before her pregnancy was visible. He'd been unhappy when she'd told him she was pregnant, even going so far as to suggest that she get an abortion so it wouldn't interrupt the shooting of his movie.

Gwen remembered that moment as if it had happened yesterday. That was when she'd no longer been able to deny that her relationship with Peter was crumbling.

Standing in the foyer of the cabin, she felt her keys slip through her trembling fingers to the floor. She glanced down at her shaking hands, spotting the engagement ring, and took a deep breath and closed her eyes. Food, she needed food. That was the reason she had the shakes, she told herself. She hadn't eaten anything since morning.

The sound of Luc's voice was muffled by the closed guest bedroom door. Relieved he wouldn't see her in her current state, she picked up her keys, shrugged out of her jacket, hung it in the hall closet and went to the kitchen to scrounge up something to eat.

Soup, she decided, pulling a can from the shelves. And peanut butter and honey sandwiches. Not exactly gourmet, but it would fill her up. She would have to toast the bread because it was frozen.

Trying to think about anything except the baby she'd lost years ago, she heated the soup and made two sandwiches just in case Luc was desperate for nourishment.

Her mind flashed back to that day on the set when she'd fallen. The private emergency room, emergency surgery, Peter insisting on complete privacy and secrecy regarding the loss of her pregnancy. Waking up and feeling empty.

"Smells good," Luc said just steps behind her.

His voice startled her, and she accidentally touched the hot pan with her fingers. Scalding pain singed her fingers, and she drew back, gasping. "Oh, no," she said.

Luc swore under his breath. "Put your hand under the water," he said, pulling her to the sink and plunging her hand under cool running water. "Damn, I didn't mean to surprise you that much," he said.

Overwhelmed by the combination of pain from her

hand and the comfort of his chest at her back, she shook her head. "It's not your fault. I was thinking about too many things at once. It's just a little accident."

"Does this happen often? Burning yourself while cooking?"

"Why?" she asked. "It's usually food I burn, not myself."

He nodded. "You get distracted."

"Yes. There are more important things than food."

"That's why you have so many frozen meals ready for the microwave."

She grimaced. "Okay, you know my secret. Well, one of them," she amended. She started to pull her hand away from the faucet. "I think I'm better—"

He shook his head. "No. Keep it submerged for another few minutes. I'll take care of the soup."

Gwen glanced over her shoulder at Luc as he removed the pot from the burner and poured soup into the two bowls she'd set on the counter. There was a total sense of unreality to this picture. She would have never imagined seeing one of the powerful Hudsons in her kitchen serving soup.

Luc looked up and met her gaze. "You're staring. Why?"

She shook her head. "It wasn't on my calendar to have Luc Hudson in my kitchen this week, or any other week."

His lips curved in a half grin. "Just lucky, I guess."

"Which one of us is lucky?" she shot back. "You or me?"

"Excellent point. On the surface, most men would give an arm or leg or both to be in my position."

"I hear a *but* coming."

"Who wouldn't want to be stuck in a cabin with the sexiest woman of 2004?"

She groaned. "Don't remind me."

"Just curious," he said, his gaze sliding over her sweater. "Do you still have that shirt?"

Feeling his gaze like a touch, she bit her lip. "No, it was just a man's shirt. Nothing special."

"Do you know how many men had fantasies about that shirt?"

She felt her cheeks heat. "No, and I don't want to know."

"Of course, the fantasies were about *removing* the shirt," he continued.

"Which didn't happen. So you can put that in the unfulfilled-fantasy column." She turned off the faucet.

"A lot of reality is about unfulfilled fantasy," he said.

"It can be," she agreed and glanced at him. "How did you learn that?"

"My position. My brothers call me a PR wizard, but I know the truth. It's all spin and semantics." He moved the bowls to the small dining room table and gestured for her to sit.

"Just a minute," she said and impulsively grabbed a bottle of wine from the refrigerator and scooped a couple of wineglasses from the cabinet. After pulling a corkscrew from a drawer, she brought the sand-wiches to the table. She sat down, thinking for a flash of a moment that his gentlemanly manners made her feel more feminine than she had in a long time. "That's part of the reason I like living here. Not much spin at all. People say what they think. I've never felt more at peace."

He nodded. "How come I haven't seen a man around to help you enjoy your newfound peace? You must have had some contenders."

She put the corkscrew on the wine bottle, and he took it from her hands. "Maybe that's part of the secret to my peace. I could ask you the same question. Isn't there a woman—" she paused and shot him a sideways glance, unable to conceal a ghost of a smile "—or *women* back in L.A. who will be devastated by the announcement of your engagement?"

He shot her his version of a sideways glance and shook his head, pulling off the cork and pouring the wine. "I haven't had a serious relationship in two years. I almost made a big mistake."

She watched him take a sip. "I bought that wine at the drugstore. The vintage is uncertain at best. But you mentioned mistakes. We all make them. How did you avoid making yours?"

"I don't run from the truth when it smacks me in the face," he said, his own face hard with cynicism. "I don't run from much of anything."

She could see that his strength was more than skin-deep. The knowledge gave her a shiver of awareness she hadn't felt in a long, long time. He aroused her curiosity and made her aware of herself as a woman.

"So, how did the 'almost' part happen?" she asked, taking a bite of her sandwich and sipping her soup.

"My brothers say I suffer from rescuing-damsel-in-distress syndrome."

She smiled. "Pregnant horses included?"

He gave a rough chuckle and met her gaze. She felt something sizzle and hum between them and glanced away. Where was this breathless feeling coming from?

"I met a woman whose car had broken down. One thing led to another. We started seeing each other. She was a part-time actress. I introduced her to some people. I was going to propose," he said. "Until I found out she'd gotten involved on the sly with a producer I'd introduced to her at a party."

Gwen grimaced. "Sorry. At least you found out before you got married. That's more than I can say. I was so young and naive, and Peter gave me the big rush. I was pretty unfocused at that point. I'd done a few commercials and some small parts. He was the exact opposite. He knew exactly what he was going to do and how to get there. He seemed to know exactly what I should do, too."

"You eventually disagreed."

Gwen thought of her pregnancy and nodded. "He was willing to sacrifice something I couldn't."

"Must have been pretty big to turn you off acting, L.A. and men."

"It was," she said, but her discomfort drove her to her feet even though she hadn't finished eating. "Um, do you want some more soup? Another sandwich?"

He circled her wrist with his fingers as she tried to step away from the table, compelling her to look at him. "I'm good, but you need to eat more. Sit down and finish."

Gwen took a deep breath, exasperated with herself. During her acting days, she had kissed major movie stars. Why did Luc Hudson bother her so much? She sank into her seat and sipped her soup and ate her sandwich, determined to finish as soon as possible.

"When we took Nicki to rehab, she told us not to call her parents. She said to call you instead," Luc said.

Gwen stopped midbite then swallowed and nodded. "My father moved to Arizona and hasn't been in touch. My mother remarried and lives in Malibu. She would be upset by the negative publicity. If it isn't good news, she doesn't want to hear it."

"Life doesn't always give you roses," he said.

"Even though you can spin it that way," she said.

"Right," he said. "Part of the reason I can spin it is because I face the hard facts head on. Our family has dealt with some tragedy. The death of my grandfather is still difficult. He was the heart, breath and soul of Hudson Pictures. We all want to live up to what he created."

"Tall order?"

"In more than business," Luc said. "He was the kind of man who could fill up a room with his personality. He had a huge passion for the business, but he also had a huge passion for my grandmother, and it never seemed to wane. He met and secretly married her during World War II in France. He founded the studio to bring her talents to the big screen. In a strange way, I think all of us are striving to find a love that matches what he and my grandmother had. Hell," he said, "he may be gone, but my grandmother still loves him."

"That's an amazing story," she said.

"Yeah, and if I weren't so damn cynical, I might

believe the same kind of thing could happen to me. Lightning that lasts."

She nodded, understanding. "Lightning that lasts," she echoed. "Maybe it's harder to be cynical when you see someone who actually had that. Then it's not a myth."

He reached his hand toward her hair and pushed a strand away from her face. "Yeah." He gazed into her eyes for a few seconds, which made her lose her breath.

"You have any cards?" he finally asked.

She glanced away so she could think. "Uh, yes, I do."

"Let's play," he said.

"What?"

"Poker. Strip poker if you're inclined," he joked in a deep voice.

"In your dreams," she said, but she had this terrifying but exhilarating sense that Luc Hudson just might have the ability to talk her out of her clothes. "I need to keep an eye on the mare via the camera."

"The same way you did last night?" he asked, raising a dark eyebrow.

Nice of him to remind her that she'd fallen asleep so soundly that she hadn't remembered his carrying her to bed. "I'm not as exhausted tonight."

"You don't really plan to stay up all night, do you?"

"No, but—"

"We can play in your office. It'll make the time pass more quickly."

He made a good point and Gwen liked card games. She had since she was a child. "Okay, but my clothes are staying on."

"Does that mean you want me to take mine off?"

The mix of humor and sensuality slipped past her defenses and sent a shimmer of awareness all the way through her body. "No," she said, although an image of Luc, naked, immediately shot through her mind, making her feel singed. "I'll get the cards."

"I'll bring the wine."

"I'll fix some coffee," she countered, thinking the combination of wine and Luc Hudson could be dangerous. She grabbed the cards and led the way into the small office. She looked at the monitor and saw the mare moving around the stall.

"She's getting stronger," Luc said from behind her.

"Yes. That means we'll probably have to let her out into the paddock soon." Gwen shuffled the cards and dealt them.

Distracted by the sight of his hands cradling his hand of cards and his long legs stretched out across from hers, she tried to concentrate on her own cards.

"Maximum bet is twenty-five cents. Maximum raise fifty cents. I bet fifteen cents. What's your favorite color?" he asked, drawing a card from the pile.

"Um, periwinkle. Why do you ask?" She looked at her cards and tried not to reveal her disappointment. "I'll see your fifteen cents."

"Because the media showing up tomorrow have decided it would be cute to give each of us a quiz about the other."

Gwen glanced away from her cards. "Media tomorrow? We just did that today. I thought the other interviews would be over the phone."

He shook his head, discarded two cards and drew two

from the pile. "I need to know everything about you, and you need to know everything about me. I'll bet twenty-five cents."

She sighed in frustration. "Okay, so blue is your favorite color," she began.

"What makes you say that?"

"When asked to name his favorite color, almost every man on the planet will say blue."

"Mine is green," he said.

"You're just being contrary," she said.

"Romantic," he countered. "Your eyes are green."

"Borderline sappy," she said, discarding and drawing.

"Where do you want to honeymoon?" he asked.

The question jolted her. "Honeymoon?"

"Tahiti or Bali?" he said, discarding and drawing.

"Somewhere more private," she mused. "Peter took me to Hawaii. I found out later that he leaked our plans to the press so they would show up to take photos."

Luc met her gaze. "Really?" he said in disbelief.

"Yeah," she said. "All about the PR."

"Not on your honeymoon," he said.

"You can't tell me that you've never exploited the honeymoon angle," she said, discarding three of her sorry cards and drawing three more sorry cards. "Check."

"Maybe, but the couples who are really in love just tell me to take a flying—" He broke off, suddenly reaching the conclusion that Gwen had reached for herself.

Silence fell between them.

"You have my sympathy," he said.

Her pride stung, she raised her chin. "Don't you dare pity me for what Peter—"

"Because you're going to lose this hand," he interjected, laying his full house on the table.

She stared at his cards then hers. One card shy of a full house, she scowled at him. "Beginner's luck," she said. "I'll get you in the next game."

He laughed. "In your dreams," he said and scooped up the cards and shuffled them. "Now you owe me."

"Owe you what?" she asked. "We were only playing for pennies."

"Pennies translate into favors," he said, shuffling again. "You wouldn't play for clothing, so it'll have to be favors."

"Favors," she echoed. "What do you call this fake engagement? Oh, wait, my mistake. That's blackmail."

"Exactly," he said, presenting the deck for her to cut it. "So we're playing for favors."

"What if I win the same number of times you do? Doesn't that just negate the winnings?"

"That won't happen," he said. "But if it did, you would get the same number of favors from me."

"What if I don't want any favors from you?"

"You will," he said, meeting her gaze for a long moment that took her breath away.

"Deal," she said, determined to teach him a lesson.

For the next two hours, they traded victories and secrets. She learned his favorite music, food, beer and pastimes, and he learned hers. It occurred to her that Luc would know more about her preferences after two days than her husband had known after three years.

"First crush?" she asked, preparing to rack up another win for herself.

"Sara Jameson, fourth grade," he said.

Gwen stared at him in surprise. "You remember her name? I would have thought you'd have dated so many women that their names would run together."

He shook his head. "If I'm the master of spin, then don't you think I know how to create it for myself?"

"Are you telling me the playboy image isn't real?"

"I create my image, then do what I want," he said.

"You didn't really answer my question," she told him.

"I told you the name of my first crush. We didn't break up until she moved away, freshman year in high school."

"Wow, that's longevity."

"What about you?"

"I was shy, too tall. It took me a while."

"You had to grow into those legs," he said, his gaze sliding over her denim-clad figure.

"Tucker Martin," she said with a sigh. "He had dimples and blue eyes. He was smart and funny."

"How long did that last?"

"Oh, it never got off the ground. He didn't notice me," she said.

He gave a bark of laughter. "Poor sap. Bet he's kicking himself down the street these days." He placed his cards on the table. "Full house, again."

She mentally swore. "You're impossible."

"I work at it," he said. "You owe me another favor."

She sighed and glanced at the monitor again. The horse had settled down. "I'll think about that tomorrow," she said quoting Scarlett O'Hara. "Time for me to go to bed." She rose and he did too, standing mere inches from her. "Thanks for the amusement."

"My pleasure. You need to give me one of my favors now," he said.

A warning instinct flashed through her. "Why?"

"It's something I need to know for the interview," he said, moving closer to her.

She should step away from him, but for just a moment, his closeness felt good. "What?"

He lowered his head closer and closer, taking her breath with each corresponding invasion of her space. "I need to know how you taste."

He gave her three agonizing seconds to protest or refuse, three seconds to turn back or pull away. But Gwen did none of those sensible things, because she wanted to know how he tasted, too.

Five

"You've already kissed me," she said against his lips, distracted by the texture of his mouth, the sensation of his chest beneath her palm.

"That didn't count," he muttered.

Her mind scrambled like electrical circuits gone haywire as he rubbed his mouth over hers. Her body instantly heated and she craved more. She couldn't remember when she'd felt this way before. Had she ever?

"You taste like honey," he said in a low voice and slid his tongue over her lips.

Instinctively opening for him, she moved closer so that her breasts pressed against his hard chest. She couldn't withhold a soft moan.

He slid his powerful thigh between hers, and she felt

a shocking spike of need. Distantly, she felt him move her against the wall. It was cool against her back, but he was so warm, so strong, so male. And somehow she knew he could take care of her sexually, maybe in every way. Was that possible?

Her emotions ran from one end of the spectrum to the other. Should she stop? Should she go further?

Luc slid his hand underneath her sweater and wrapped his hand around her waist. The sensation of his hand on her bare skin sent her equilibrium in to a tailspin.

She slipped her hands up to his head, giving in to the urge to plunge her fingers through his hair. His groan was gratifying, and he brushed his hard masculinity against her. Sucking his tongue deeper into her mouth, she savored his taste, savored the sensation of him.

Luc slid one of his hands down to her bottom, guiding her against his hardness while he skimmed his other hand up her rib cage to just below her breasts.

She held her breath, dying for his touch. Her nipples strained against her bra. She fought the forbidden urge to pull off her sweater and feel her naked breasts against his bare chest. Her heart pounded against her ribs.

She felt his hand slide to her back and felt the catch of her bra release. One. Two. Three seconds later, she felt his palm cupping her breast.

Gwen sighed against his mouth.

His thumb brushed her nipple and she gasped.

"You feel so good. So good," he said, French kissing her again.

He rocked inside the cradle of her thighs, sending a shower of sensations firing through her bloodstream.

She was shocked by the carnal need he drew out of her. Images of their bodies, naked and hot, writhing together, singed her mind. She could taste his wanting, his need.

His hand slid underneath her jeans and panties, grasping her naked bottom at the same time she felt him caressing her breast.

"Oh, my—" He broke off and thrust his tongue into her mouth.

His heat pumped up her heat. She gave in to the urge to slide her hands beneath his sweater and feel his smooth, sleek skin.

"You make me so hot," he said against her mouth and swore. "I haven't gotten this worked up since I was a teenager."

She rippled against him, desperately seeking more.

He slid one of his hands between them. Seconds passed and he guided her hand down to touch him intimately. He was large and hard. She stroked him, driven by his desire, by her desire to please him.

His breath caught, and she loved that he was just as affected as she was.

"Are you sure you want this?"

His voice whispered over her like a warm California breeze. *Did she want this? Should she? How crazy was this?*

"Too fast," she said breathlessly when a drop of rational thinking trickled into her brain. She pushed away from him and shook her head. "Too crazy. I'm sorry. I shouldn't have—"

He covered her mouth with his hand. "No apologies," he said, and she was compelled to look at him.

She felt the searing connection with him again, and fought it, again.

"We'll be lovers," he said with a confidence that should have sounded arrogant but instead was just rock-hard certain. "It's just a matter of time." He lowered his head and brushed his lips over her cheek. "Sweet dreams, Gwen," he said and walked away.

Gwen stood there for several breathless seconds. "Oh, wow," she whispered and slid her fingers through her hair, clutching her head and closing her eyes. She racked her brain for when she'd felt this way before, but her brain would produce nothing.

She and Luc were from different worlds now. She should not give in to temptation, but she didn't know if she could let him pass by. The combination of his honor and his pragmatic understanding of Hollywood that meshed with the masculinity and power he emanated fascinated her. Gwen had the feeling that once she gave herself to him, she would never be the same, and she wasn't sure what her world would look like after she made love with him. Should she resist? Could she?

The next morning, Luc joined Gwen as she cared for the horses. She spent extra time with the expectant mare, now known as Pyrrha.

Pyrrha pricked up her ears when Luc stood at the door to her stall, and she walked toward him. "Hello, beautiful," he said to her, holding out his palm.

Pyrrha whinnied and allowed him to stroke her. Feeling Gwen's gaze on him, Luc looked at her. Irritation furrowed her lovely face. "Problem?" he asked.

"I can't believe it," she said.

"What?"

"Even the horse recognizes that whole alpha thing in you," she said.

"Smart horse," he said and grinned.

She met his gaze and clearly tried, very hard, not to smile. Her lips twitched and she began to laugh. "You're terrible."

"I can show you terrible," he said, ready to show her.

She inhaled quickly and glanced away, looking at Pyrrha. "She's looking much better. The vet says the baby's heartbeat is strong. I just hope we can keep her happy during her confinement."

"I'm sure you'll have to name that foal, so you may as well start planning."

Gwen sighed and met his gaze. "You make it seem possible."

She made him want to make her believe in a lot of things. Himself. Herself. Luc wondered if his knight instinct was kicking in. It didn't matter. He wanted her and was determined to have her.

Three hours later, a crew from Entertainment TV showed up with cameras and a reporter. The reporter, a brunette named Trina with big breasts and hair extensions, appeared torn between her awe of Gwen and her hopes of making an impression on Luc for career purposes.

After a few general questions, Trina gave a huge smile. "I've saved the best for last. I want to ask Gwen some questions about you and ask you some questions about Gwen. We'll see who wins," Trina said. "Mr. Hudson, go amuse yourself while I ask Gwen some questions."

"What do you mean?" Gwen asked.

"I don't want Mr. Hudson to hear your answers until he has answered the same questions. You can go out on the front porch," Trina said. "This shouldn't take long."

Considering the temperature was hovering at nine degrees that day, he hoped it wouldn't. For a second, he wondered if Gwen would be able to keep up their charade without his presence as a reminder.

She reached out to take his hand and pulled him toward her. Kissing his cheek, she smiled into his eyes as if she really meant it. "Don't worry, sweetheart. I won't reveal too many of your terrible secrets."

His gut tightened at her playful, seductive expression, and he forced himself to remember that he was staring into the face of an Academy Award–nominated actress. Luc had learned that *actress* was another word for *liar*. Gwen would be fine with Trina.

Throwing on a jacket, hat and gloves, Luc wandered outside to brave the elements. Despite the cold temperature, the sun shone brightly. He walked down the steps of the porch into the yard. Snow crunched beneath his boots.

He inhaled a deep breath and felt the chilly air sweep throughout him. Although the temperature left a lot to be desired, the sound of complete quiet soothed him. No traffic, no office sounds, no senseless chatter. Just quiet and peace.

Gwen made a good point. This place offered something more rare than diamonds. He stood there for several moments and just soaked it in.

"Mr. Hudson?" one of the cameramen called from the doorway. "Trina is ready for you now."

Struck by the contrast of the purity of Gwen's sur-roundings and the lies they were fashioning inside her home, he felt a twist of the same resentment Gwen had expressed when he'd told her the press would be invading her house.

Returning to the house, he sat down and answered Trina's mostly inane questions. Then the entertainment reporter ambushed him. "What made you fall in love with Gwen?"

He paused a half beat, since he hadn't formed a prepared response for this question. Then he went with his gut. "You can look at her and see how beautiful she is. That's obvious. But that's attraction, not love. She has amazing depth and humility. At the same time she can make me laugh. When I'm with her, the world is better than I thought it could be."

Complete silence followed for a full moment. Luc glanced at Gwen, standing just a few feet away. He caught an unguarded expression of surprise and longing on her face. He felt the same emotions echo inside him.

Trina put her hand to her chest and gave a big sigh. "How romantic," she said, snapping him out of his weird emotional state.

He shook his head at himself. This was insane. Sex was one thing, but these other feelings were crazy. The deso-lation of his environment must be getting to him. Gwen joined him by his side, sliding her hand over his shoulder.

Luc stood, ready for the reporter and cameramen to leave. "Thank you for coming," he said. "Let me know when it airs."

Trina also stood and raised crossed fingers. "Tomorrow night if everything goes okay and we can't scrounge up any emergency scandals." She shot Luc a coy look. "There will be a little surprise for you, too," she said.

"Really," he said, cautious. Luc had learned not to like surprises when it came to the press.

Gwen squeezed his shoulder reassuringly. "Don't worry. She's just teasing you."

When Trina and the cameramen left, Gwen closed the door behind them and turned to meet Luc's gaze. "I thought you said you weren't much of an actor. You did pretty well with that last question Trina pulled on you."

"I've had a lot of practice thinking on my feet," he said. "I just answered the question as if I were a man who believed in real love for myself. As if I were a man who had fallen in love with you."

She gave a wry smile and walked toward him. "Sounds like acting to me."

"It wasn't that difficult," he said, unable to take his eyes off her.

She visibly inhaled. "For some reason, it's getting easier for me to pretend that I'm attracted to you."

He chuckled. "That's because you're not pretending," he said. "You *are* attracted to me just as I'm attracted to you. There's something between us. I didn't expect it, and I'm betting you didn't either, but it doesn't erase the fact that it's there."

"Lust, sex," she said.

He gave in to the urge to pull her against him. "We'll figure it out."

* * *

The following day a delivery truck arrived while Luc was on the phone, arranging for publicity for another Hudson movie. He walked to the door and noticed Gwen returning from the barn to the house. She stared at the truck, then at him.

"Just a few things since I'm going to be here for another week and a half," he said. The driver began to unload several large boxes.

Gwen scooted past the driver and looked at the boxes suspiciously. "What things?" she asked.

"While I'm beginning to appreciate the peacefulness of your surroundings, your technology is archaic," he said. "That television is at least ten years old, and your Internet is too slow." No sooner had the driver finished bringing in the boxes when Luc spotted a van turning into the long driveway.

"Roberts Satellite and Television Setup." Gwen read the words on the side of the van, staring at him in disbelief. "Have you lost your mind? We already have
satellite TV."

"This is better, more powerful, more stations."

"I don't need more stations," she said.

"I do. Football, basketball," he said.

"Oh, this is ridiculous. I'm afraid to ask the size of the dishes. You just need to remember to take all this stuff with you when you leave."

"No problem," he said. "But I bet you'll want to keep them. Once you get used to having something good, you don't want to give it up. Speaking of something good, two of those boxes contain food. Do you mind unpacking them while I deal with the satellite guy?"

"Food," she said, her eyes rounding. She opened her mouth in protest and seemed to think better of it. She bit her lip. "Are you saying you don't want peanut butter sandwiches and soup every night?"

"Do you?"

"Okay, okay," she grumbled, and began to open the food boxes.

Hours later, with the new widescreen TV ready for action, Luc turned on the set just before Entertainment TV was scheduled. He would study the interview to see what adjustments he and Gwen would need to make for future appearances.

He glanced around for Gwen but didn't see her. "Gwen," he called. "We need to watch the interview."

"I'm watching Pyrrha," she called from her office. "She seems a little restless."

Frowning, he walked to her office doorway. "Take a break from it. We need to study the interview to remember what's been said and to plan for the next one."

"I remember what I said," she replied, her eyes glued to her computer screen.

"Yes, but you need to remember what I said, too," he said, moving closer and glancing over her shoulder. "Pyrrha is eating. She looks fine."

Kicking her foot in what looked like a case of nerves, she met his gaze. "I don't like to watch my performances."

He'd heard this before, but he wondered what the nerves were about. "This is different. It's an interview."

"Still a performance," she said.

He spun her chair around and looped his hand around her wrist and dragged her out of the chair. "It won't last that long."

"I really don't—"

An uneasy suspicion grew in Luc's gut as he tugged her down on the couch in front of the television. "What exactly did you tell that reporter?"

She shrugged but evaded his gaze. "I just did my part to add a little kick to the proceedings."

His suspicion roared. "What the hell—"

"She may not even use it," Gwen said.

"Gwen?" he said in a quiet voice that he reserved as an unmistakable warning of his displeasure.

She bit her lip but shook her head. "If you're going to make me sit here and watch it, then you're just going to have to wait and see it for yourself."

"I don't like surprises," he said.

"We're even. I don't like watching myself on the screen. Any screen."

A photo of Luc and Gwen flashed across the screen, interrupting their discussion. "Stay tuned. Our very own Trina Troy braved the cold Montana mountains to get the hot lowdown on movie star turned horse rescuer Gwen McCord and Hudson Pictures' hottest bachelor of the moment, Luc Hudson," said the cheery host of Entertainment TV.

"Do you think Trina Troy is a real name?" Gwen asked.

"No chance," he muttered and brooded for a long moment.

Both rose almost in unison.

"I'm getting a be—"

"I'm getting a glass of wine."

They both spoke at once.

Gwen shot a quick, uneasy smile and squeezed past him to the refrigerator. He followed her to the fridge, and she pulled out a beer and thrust it into his hand. "Here."

"You seem a little jumpy," he said.

She grabbed a bottle of wine and poured a glass. "I'd forgotten how intense the paparazzi can be. Or maybe I just chose to forget." She took a sip and licked her lips. "I'm also not used to having someone around the house all the time."

Luc found his attention snagged by the sight of her pink tongue sliding over her lips. He pushed back a stray strand of her hair just because he wanted to touch her. "Am I bothering you?"

She took another quick sip. "Bother." She rolled the word around her mouth as if to test it. "Yes," she said. "And you should stop it right away."

He chuckled. "Can't do that. In fact, I plan to bother you more."

She shot him a dark, sexy look that almost distracted him from the shrill voice of the Entertainment TV reporter.

"We're back now with Trina Troy, who is going to tell us how Luc Hudson is keeping Gwen McCord hot under the covers during those cold Montana nights."

Luc shot a quick glance at the screen, then looked at Gwen. "Hot under the covers?" he echoed, catching her hand and tugging her toward the sofa.

"Not my words," she said.

"Entertainment TV paid a visit to Luc Hudson and

Gwen McCord at her Montana ranch. The two love-birds were willing to play a little game of favorite things with me."

The tape played, showing Gwen smiling as she answered the reporter's questions about Luc's favorites. The camera, as usual, loved her, catching her expressions of delight and a tinge of shyness. Her hair shimmered and her skin glowed. She looked like a woman in love. She played the part so well he could almost believe her himself.

"This could be the real deal. Look at what Luc Hudson has to say about Gwen," Trina said, introducing the shot of him talking about what had made him fall in love with Gwen.

He bought his line, surprised at the way the camera caught the chemistry between him and Gwen.

"We asked Gwen the same question, and she said Luc has a deep-seated sense of honor that won her over. But look at what else she said."

"Here it comes," Gwen murmured and took another sip of wine.

The film played. "What made me fall in love with Luc?" Gwen echoed and tilted her head to one side as if she were concentrating on the question. "Besides the obvious superficial things such as how hot he is and how his great body comes in handy for a lot of things including rescuing horses and picking me up when I fall." She gave a sexy chuckle. "There's the fact that he is amazing in bed," she said. "Amazing."

Shocked, Luc turned to look at Gwen. "What in hell—"

"I had to stall," she said, shrugging helplessly. "That question wasn't on the list. I wasn't prepared for it. And you know what they say. Sex sells."

His cell phone began to ring and he swore. "Do you realize how much heat I'm going to take for this? My family, my business associates." He picked up the phone and spit out his name. "Luc Hudson."

"Mr. Hudson, I'm with *Hottie Magazine*, and we wondered if you would consider doing a centerfold spread for—"

"No, but thank you very much," he said and turned off the phone. He turned to Gwen as she attempted to ease her way out of the room. "Not so fast. You've just created my headache of the week."

"Sorry," she said with a slight wince. "But you did say you wanted a distraction from Nicki's problems, and…" Her voice trailed off as he walked toward her.

"And?" he said.

She gave a nervous chuckle. "And better you than me."

Six

Better you than me.

Seeing the light of challenge in Luc's eyes, Gwen immediately got the uneasy feeling she'd made a big mistake.

"Maybe we'll just have to make sure you know what you're talking about when you describe me as 'amazing in bed,'" he said, brushing his muscular body against her.

Gwen felt a ridiculous weakening in her knees and tried to stiffen them.

Luc met her gaze, then leisurely glanced down her body the same way she imagined he would move his hands over her. He made her burn, just by looking.

He raised his finger to her cheek, skimmed it down to her mouth and lingered there before he slid that same

finger over her chin and down her throat to \
pulse raced.

"Why is your heart beating so fast?" he asked in a
low, mocking voice that made her nerve endings over-
sensitive. He dipped his finger still lower between her
breasts. "You're breathing fast, too. Signs of arousal?"

The way he touched her tempted her. She liked the
feeling of his hand on her, the promise it made, the
promise his eyes made. He was so solidly male, and he
made her more sensually aware of herself than ever
before. He made her aware of her femininity deeper
than just in her skin, or even into her bones, it seemed
to permeate to a cellular level.

How could this be anything but a big mistake? She
took a deep breath. Fighting the urge to give in to her
own urges, she grabbed his wrist and stared at it. His skin
was darker than hers, his hands much larger. His muscles
flexed beneath hers, but he didn't pull away from her.

"I don't want to be stupid," she whispered.

"I will make you feel a lot of things, Gwen. Stupid
isn't one of them."

She took another deep breath, willing the need to go
further with him to lessen. It didn't, but she was relieved
that he wouldn't use her weakness for him against her.

"I won't take you until you're ready, but soon
enough, you will be," he said.

That should have sounded arrogant as hell, but Gwen
was too close to the edge, too full of wanting to deny
the truth. She withdrew her hand from around his wrist
and took a step back. She desperately needed the space.
"I—uh—I should go check on Pyrrha."

He nodded with a knowing expression on his face. "You know where to find me."

Her heart still hammering in her chest, she felt as if she were looking her fate in the eye. She tore her gaze from his and fled to her office, closing the door behind her. She didn't want this complication in her life right now. She didn't want to feel this way for a man who was so much a part of the life she'd left behind.

Torn in opposing directions, she looked at the monitor and did a double take. She narrowed her eyes at the screen. "What—" she muttered under her breath, checking for a different view of Pyrrha's stall, then another.

Her blood ran cold. Oh, no, it couldn't be. It couldn't— "Luc," she yelled, frantic, bursting through the door. "She's gone, Luc. Pyrrha is gone."

She and Luc immediately started to search. Dennis instructed them to stay in touch and said he would bring the horse trailer as soon as they called him. It turned out that the barn help hadn't completely closed the door to Pyrrha's stall and the horse had literally walked out the door.

It was pitch-black, bitter cold, and snow fell sideways owing to the raging wind.

Luc decided to use an ATV to follow Gwen's Lab, June, as the dog searched for Pyrrha's scent. Gwen was worried out of her mind. "She wasn't ready for this," she said to Luc. "She hadn't rested enough. Her scrapes hadn't healed."

"We'll find her," he said, focusing on the dark, icy terrain.

"How can you be sure?"

"Because we're both too hardheaded not to find her," he said and spared her a quick glance.

His confidence quieted her panic to a dull roar inside her. It felt as if they were crawling behind June. Every moment seemed to take forever.

After an hour, Luc gave June some water and put slippers on the dog to protect her paws. Their breath left visible vapor trails in the air. He turned to Gwen. "It's too cold out here. I'll call Dennis to take you back to the house."

She shook her head vehemently. "No, I'm okay."

"Gwen—"

She shook her head again. "Really, I'm okay. Being beside you is keeping me warm," she admitted.

"Okay," he conceded reluctantly. "A little longer."

They continued on for another twenty-five minutes and Luc stopped the ATV. He touched her cold nose. "I can't let you stay out here any longer."

"I'm f-fi—" She broke off, appalled that her chattering teeth revealed how chilled she was.

"That's it," he said.

June raced ahead, barking loudly.

Gwen's heart raced in hope. "She's f-found something. We have to follow her."

Luc followed the lab to a small wooded area and killed the engine. He helped Gwen out of the ATV and grabbed a rope and halter. "You sure you can do this?"

She nodded emphatically, but silently, because she didn't want him to hear her teeth chattering again. Stepping into the footsteps he created in the snow, she followed him into the woods. June continued to bark, and she could hear a scrambling sound.

"Sounds like June has cornered something," Luc said.

Less than a moment later, they heard a neigh. He stopped to listen, and another neigh sounded. Glancing back at Gwen, he nodded with a smile and offered her his hand. "That dog deserves a steak when we get back."

"Sh-she'll get it," Gwen said, hanging on to Luc as he picked up his pace. Meandering through the trees, they stopped when they found Pyrrha trapped between two trees with a stone wall at her back and June guarding her escape. Gwen immediately called Dennis on her cell phone to give him their location.

"Ho," Luc said and approached the horse.

Pyrrha pricked up her ears at the sound of his voice. Gwen held her breath, fearing the horse would bolt and run.

Talking in a soothing voice, Luc continued his steady approached and lifted the halter to her nose. Pyrrha backed away, but her hindquarters quickly encountered the wall.

Pulling an apple from his pocket, Luc offered the fruit to Pyrrha. She tentatively walked forward, sniffing. Gwen watched in amazement as the horse took the apple from his hand. He'd known exactly how to handle the wild, frightened horse. She couldn't help wondering if his instincts extended to human women, specifically her. Luc tossed the rope over Pyrrha's head.

Relief gushed through Gwen like a waterfall. Even though she knew they still had to get Pyrrha safely back to the barn, she had a strong sense that the horse would be okay.

* * *

An hour later they had settled Pyrrha into her stall with fresh hay, fresh water and a warming light. Maybe it was crazy how she continued to identify with the pregnant horse, but Gwen felt more protective of Pyrrha and her baby than ever.

Luc moved beside her. "Dennis says the vet will visit in the morning. You should go back to the house and get some rest."

She shook her head. "I'm sleeping right here tonight. I've got a cot."

"You're crazy. I bet you're dehydrated. You're just setting yourself up to get sick."

"I'll be okay. I'm stronger than I look," she said and smiled. "My teeth stopped chattering within five minutes of when we arrived at the barn."

He gave a sigh of disapproval. "Okay, have it your way. I'll stay, too."

Strange feelings trickled through her. Gwen had been counting on some time away from Luc to regain her sense and defenses. At the moment, she was overwhelmed with all kinds of emotions—gratitude, vulnerability…and a craving to be close to him that she knew she should ignore.

"That's not necessary," she said. "Besides, there's only one cot and I'm using it."

He shrugged. "I know you have some extra blankets and sleeping bags because I saw them in the storage room."

Her energy seeping out of her with each passing moment, she raised her hands. "Okay, but don't blame me when you end up with a backache."

* * *

Luc grabbed the cot, along with a couple of sleeping bags and blankets, and brought them next to Pyrrha's stall. He joined Gwen at the stall door. She was leaning against the side, her head already bobbing from fatigue. "You're doing it again," he said in a low voice, skimming his finger underneath her chin.

Her eyelids fluttered open, and she jerked her head upward. "I'm fine. I'm not—"

"Let's take turns. You rest, I'll watch."

She rubbed her eyes with a weary motion. "I should say no. She's not your responsibility."

Luc couldn't explain why he felt protective of both Gwen and Pyrrha, but their combination of defiance and vulnerability got under his skin. "Just rest."

Hesitant, she glanced at Pyrrha, then back at him. "You're sure?"

"Yeah, I'm sure."

Her eyes softened, making his gut do strange things. "Thanks," she said. "For everything."

"No problem," he said and locked gazes with her for a moment. The hint of longing in her eyes echoed inside him.

Deliberately looking away, she turned to the cot, spread out a sleeping bag on top and crawled inside it. Her moan sounded sensual even though he knew she was dead tired and she wasn't making the sound from sexual pleasure.

Within seconds, he heard her breathing soften to the rhythm of sweet sleep. He took the opportunity to study her while she slept and felt like a thief.

He looked at her stubborn chin and wondered if her marriage to Peter Horrigan was what had made her so independent minded. She resisted his help at nearly every turn. He wondered what it would be like to have her trust. Luc sensed that Gwen's trust would be a precious thing, her love even more so.

Love? Where had that thought come from? Frowning, he looked away, glancing at Pyrrha. The horse's head dipped as she snoozed. "I bet you're tired," he murmured. "You caused some excitement tonight."

Her eyes flickered open and she looked around, then gazed at Luc; then she closed her eyes again. Luc had the odd sense that the horse trusted him, and it gave him an even odder sense of satisfaction that he hadn't felt in a long time.

He glanced at Gwen again. She was easy to watch. She would be easy to hold, but holding wouldn't be enough. Luc wanted her in the most primitive way possible, and soon enough he would have her in his bed.

Gwen felt as if she were trying to swim up from deep in the ocean. She could see the surface, but something kept her from breaking through. She blinked her eyes and finally awakened, fighting a spurt of panic. It took her a full moment to figure out where she was and why. The barn, she realized, inhaling the fresh scent of hay.

She glanced toward Pyrrha's stall and saw Luc keeping watch, a half-empty bottle of water propped on top of the door. From this angle, his broad shoulders and height were more emphasized than ever. Something inside her calmed as she looked at him.

Inhaling deeply, she slid out of her sleeping bag. Luc turned toward her and raised his finger to his mouth in a signal for her to remain silent, then extended his hand to her. Curious, she accepted his hand, quietly moved beside him and looked inside the stall.

Pyrrha was sleeping on her side in the stall.

Gwen stared at the horse in amazement. She knew that horses wouldn't lie down unless they felt safe or one of the other horses from the herd was watching over them.

She met Luc's gaze and moved her lips in a silent *Wow*. He nodded with a slight smile on his face. She pointed to her watch and mouthed, *How long*?

"About thirty minutes," he whispered.

Gwen watched the horse giving in to total rest and drank in the moment of pure peace. Luc slid his arm around her, inviting her to lean against him, and she did. Rubbing her cheek against his jacket, nestled in his embrace, she couldn't remember a time when everything in the world had felt more right.

As if they both knew how extraordinary this moment was, she and Luc stood in silence for the next quarter of an hour. Pyrrha finally stirred and rose to her feet. She looked in Luc's direction, as if to make sure he'd kept watch over her, then strolled around her stall.

"Amazing," Gwen said.

"Yeah," he said, nodding. "I'm starting to understand why you like it here."

"Totally different from L.A."

"It's all boiled down to the basics," he said, turning toward her and sifting his fingers through her hair.

His gaze wrapped around her with a primitive possessiveness, and she felt an echoing need inside her. Her heart pounded against her rib cage and she spread her hands over his hard chest, relishing his strength. She knew his strength went deeper than sinewy muscle and bone. There was something in his manner, in his spirit.

He slowly lowered his head, giving her every opportunity to turn away, and took her lips with his. Gwen sighed in relief at the sensation of his mouth on hers, firm yet sensual, taking yet giving. Three heartbeats later, she wanted more.

He pulled his mouth from hers and rubbed it over her hair. He slid one of his hands beneath her open jacket down to the small of her back and pulled her lower body against his. His arousal felt so right against her. He felt so right.

She felt a boundary inside her rip from one end to the other and raised her hands to cradle his head as she drew his mouth to hers.

He crushed her mouth with his, sliding his tongue inside, seeking and seducing. Wanting to feel all of him at once, she grasped for his back, pulling him closer. He made a barely audible growl that vibrated in her mouth.

Pulling back, he looked down at her, his nostrils flaring. "Don't start anything you don't want to finish," he said.

She sucked in a shallow breath, waiting for her defenses to rise like stone walls. But the only thing she felt was pure want and need. She wanted him more than she feared his destruction of her.

"I'm not," she finally said, then issued her own challenge. "What about you?"

His eyes widened slightly at her dare, and he lifted

her in his arms. "I'm ready for everything you want to give me."

Her mouth went desert-dry at the blatant sexual intent in his eyes.

Carrying her to the sleeping bag on the floor, he laid her down, then followed. Taking her mouth in a mind-blowing carnal kiss, he pulled off her jacket and sweater. Her bra seemed to dissolve beneath his hands. She felt a wisp of cool breeze, but he quickly covered her with his body and hands.

Desperate for the sensation of his naked skin, she pulled at his jacket and shirt. He helped her by shrugging off the layers. His golden skin was smoothly muscled and warm. He lowered his hard chest to her breasts, and a sigh of gratification sizzled from both their mouths.

He lowered his mouth to her breasts and an explosive need rocked through her. Undulating beneath him, she slipped her hands between them, tugging at his jeans.

He swore under his breath and rolled to the side so they could finish undressing each other. After he'd shoved down her jeans, he barely let a second pass before covering her again with his body.

"I want to touch you everywhere at once," he muttered against her throat as he caressed his way down to her breasts. He drew one of her nipples into his mouth at the same time that he slid his fingers between her legs, immediately finding where she was wet and swollen for him.

"You feel so good. Got to have you," he said and pushed her legs far apart. Lifting her hands above her head, he stared at her for a moment, and she felt as if lightning snapped between them.

Aching for all of him, she lifted her hips and he thrust inside her, filling her completely. She was still for a moment, absorbing the exquisite intimacy of his flesh encased in hers. She felt as if her very soul was entwined with his.

Then he began to rock in a delicious rhythm that took her higher and higher. The coil of excruciating tension inside her grew tighter with each breath she took. She moved in echoing counterpart to his thrusts. When he bent down and his chest meshed with hers and he took her mouth in a kiss, her heart and body were overwhelmed. She went up and over the edge, convulsing in waves of pleasure.

A heartbeat later, he took one last searing thrust and his release shook his powerful body, sending a vibration all the way to her core.

Their harsh breaths were the only sound in the quiet barn. Gwen's heart and mind raced. No man had ever inspired such passion in her, not even her ex-husband. Neither had she ever felt such a bone-deep connection with another human being.

The reality thrilled her at the same time that it terrified her. Suddenly she was sure of nothing except the fact that Luc Hudson had blown her safe little world to smithereens.

Seven

Luc rolled to his side and pulled Gwen flush against him. His blood finally traveled from his crotch to his brain. That had been stupid as hell. Sure, he'd been determined to have her, but he hadn't planned to take her without protection. A woman like Gwen, she had to be on the Pill, he thought. She was too beautiful, too sexual not to have a backup plan. Surely she'd had other men since her divorce….

The idea left a bitter taste in his mouth. Irrational, he told himself. Enjoy the moment. Enjoy the woman. She was different. Good different. He slid his fingers through her silky hair and relished the sensation of her breasts against his chest, her breath on his throat. He wanted her again.

He reined in his carnal urges. Barely. "As pleasurable as this was and as much as I want to repeat it immediately, I'd rather have you in a real bed."

She gave a low husky chuckle that tickled his skin and wiggled against him. "Not a bad idea. I'm with you. A mattress is much better than the ground. Maybe it's something about turning thirty."

"Speak for yourself. I got over sleeping on the floor by the time I turned twenty-five."

"That's because you're a spoiled Hudson," she said, rubbing her face against his chest as if she couldn't resist drowning herself in him.

Something in his gut twisted. "I'm not spoiled. I work my ass off."

She slid her hand over his bottom. "Feels like it's still there to me," she said in a wicked voice.

He gave a short laugh and tilted her head up so he could look into her green gaze. "You are amazing."

She bit her lip and closed her eyes, then opened them again. "Who, me?"

He shook his head. "How can you not know? You've been named sexiest woman of the year."

She pulled back slightly. "Is that why you wanted me?"

"No," he said without hesitation. "I want you—" He broke off and shook his head. "I can't even say all the reasons. For a man who makes his living knowing the right things to say, that's crazy, isn't it?"

She exhaled and leaned against him as if she trusted him. "That sexiest woman of the year was wearing a ton of makeup and fake eyelashes for that photo shoot. They put highlighter on the tops of my boobs and positioned me so I squeezed my breasts together to create more cleavage. Fake tan and highlighter on my thighs. Fake me. This is the real me."

"I like it," he said. "I want more. If you keep looking at me like that, I'll forget that we're lying on sleeping bags in a barn and I'll take you again."

She ran her tongue over his lips in a provocative motion that made him grow harder. "Would that be so bad?"

Swearing under his breath, he pulled her on top of him and positioned her over his aching hardness. She slid down, taking him fully inside her.

He moaned in pleasure. Sliding his hands over her round derriere, he flexed his pelvis upward. She sank down and rose above him, then slid down again.

Her breasts brushed his chest. He wanted more, more more…. She rose again, her breasts swaying inches from his face. Reaching upward, he took one of her nipples into his mouth. She tasted so sweet and felt like liquid sex, squeezing him, milking him.

He gave in to the erotic motion, devouring her shudders of pleasure, plunging into her. It didn't take long before the tension inside him became almost painful.

She kept riding him, and it was as if she was determined to squeeze his release from him with her delicious velvet femininity. Luc arched against her in a mind-blowing climax. He should have been done. But he wanted more of her.

The next morning Gwen awakened from a short nap with gritty eyes and a sense of being alive that she hadn't felt in forever. She turned over the care of Pyrrha to a trusted worker and arranged for a sign to be posted instructing that the mare's door remain shut. On the way back to the house, Luc's cell phone began to ring. After listening to the caller, he shot Gwen a dark look.

"Thank you, but no. I'm not an actor and never wanted to be. I wish you every success with your film, *Naked Bachelors of L.A.* Goodbye." He turned to Gwen and shook his head. "At this rate I may to need to hire a publicist for my—"

His cell rang again and he swore under his breath. "Luc Hudson," he said in a terse voice. "Thank you, but no. I'm not interested in writing a how-to book on sexual techniques for men. Goodbye."

Wincing, Gwen stepped up her pace, but Luc caught her from behind and pulled her against him. "You have caused a lot of trouble for me."

Unable to keep herself from giggling, she turned to face him and shrugged. "I was just telling the truth. You can't blame me for that."

His gaze darkened, and the intimacy they'd shared hovered between them. "I could say the same about you, but I wouldn't want men dying in Montana blizzards while they beat a path to get to you."

She shook her head at the ridiculous suggestion. "I'm sorry. I didn't realize it would cause so much trouble."

"I'll forward this line to my assistant and use another cell phone for a while. I'll just tell them I'm busy with my fiancée," he said with a sexy chuckle. "How do you plan to keep me busy?"

Her heart skipped over itself at the expression on his face. She could think of lots of ways they could keep each other busy, and all of them made her feel hot even though the current temperature was in the single digits. Unsure of what she was dealing with, she pulled on a straight face. "We have a lot of manure that needs to be shoveled."

"You witch," he said, pulling her off her feet and throwing her onto his shoulder. He marched to the house. "I'll show you how to keep me busy."

Despite his lack of sleep, Luc would have taken Gwen straight to bed if his cell phone hadn't rung again. He almost hit the ignore button before he saw Devlin's cell number on the caller ID. "It's my brother," he said to Gwen. "I should take it."

"I'll take a shower," she said.

"Hey, Dev," he said.

Devlin started right in. "What the hell—"

"You told me to take care of the Nicki McCord problem. That's what I'm doing."

"And this stuff about Gwen McCord saying you're hell on wheels in bed? Was that part of the plan?"

Dev always cringed whenever personal information about the family was leaked. He didn't want anything affecting the bottom line he so carefully protected. "You're just jealous that it's not you," he said.

A pause followed. "I have my own projects. Just make sure the Hudsons don't look like a joke. That's never good for business."

Luc shrugged out of his jacket and pulled off his hat. "It wasn't planned," he admitted. "She did it as a joke. But as long as I downplay it, I figure it will just add to our mythical status."

"Are you saying she doesn't have intimate knowledge? Because heaven help us if she gets desperate for money and decides to sell an exposé on her sexual fling with the Hudsons."

"She couldn't be less interested in doing an exposé. She's focused on this horse-rescue operation," Luc said.

"Sounds like she's sold you," Dev said. "You're not getting sucked into another rescue scheme, are you?"

"I appreciate your brotherly concern, but I can handle this."

A long silence followed. "Okay," Dev said. "Just one more thing. Is she as beautiful as she used to be?"

"More," Luc said.

Dev chuckled. "Maybe you could talk her into making a comeback with Hudson Pictures."

"She says she's not interested."

"They all say that, but when the right role is offered…"

Luc shrugged. "We'll see."

"Okay, you'll be bringing her back to L.A. in a week or so, won't you?"

"That's the plan," he said but felt conflicted about it. He felt as if he'd just discovered the Garden of Eden, and he wasn't inclined to leave it. "I'll talk to you later."

"Later, hot pants," Dev said and hung up.

Luc rolled his eyes and turned his cell phone to Silent. He needed to think, and a shower was a good place to start. He walked to the bathroom, ditched his clothes and turned on the shower.

Stepping in front of the hot spray, he did what came naturally to him. He put together a strategy for him and Gwen. She was like honey in his hands, and he had no intention of staying away from her. She must be attracted to him, because of the way she responded to him. Whatever was happening between them felt explosive, but they weren't kids. This could be controlled.

Gwen rubbed the towel over her wet hair, trying to rub some sense into her head. Had she lost her mind? Literally *hitting the hay* with Hollywood's hottest PR man.

Maybe a fling was just what she needed. Except it didn't feel the same way a fling should. The attraction was too deep. Sure, Luc's body was amazing, and the way he had made love to her had taken her to a whole new level of pleasure, but…

Swearing under her breath, she dipped her head forward, picked up her blow-dryer and began to dry her hair, her mind spinning a mile a minute. Maybe they should stop now. After all, this entire situation, combined with a fake engagement, added up to pure insanity.

"Crazy, crazy, crazy," she whispered to herself. She turned her head and her gaze encountered a pair of feet and muscular calves beneath a white towel. Of its own volition, her gaze rose, encountering a white towel slung low over narrow hips, a white scar slashed across tanned skin, a washboard abdomen, breathtaking pecs and well-defined arms.

She met his gaze and dropped the blow-dryer.

"Whoa," he said, picking it up and turning it off. "Sorry I startled you."

She pulled her cozy yellow robe more tightly around her. "You did," she said, her gaze slipping to his chest again. She dragged her eyes to meet his. "Surprise me."

"I thought you might be backtracking—second-, third-guessing what we did last night," he said. "Repeatedly."

"Well, I was thinking," she confessed.

"Believe it or not, I can do enough of that for both of us," he said and raked his hand through his hair.

"Really?" she said, surprised.

"Yeah. I didn't come to Montana with the intent to seduce you."

She didn't reply.

"But once I was around you, I wanted you."

"I wanted you, too, but—"

"No buts," he said, raising his hand. "We shared something amazing last night. I haven't felt that way in a long time. Have you?"

Not ever, she thought but wasn't ready to confess it. "No."

He put his hands over her arms. "Then I don't want to miss this with you because of the way it started."

"You mean as blackmail."

"You can look at it that way."

"There's another way?"

"You need something from me. I need something from you."

She closed her eyes and inhaled, trying to think. "So is this a fling? An affair?"

"I don't know. Let's find out."

She opened her eyes, and his honesty shook her. He could have made false promises or created a vision of an impossibly happy ending.

"I want you. You want me. It's more than physical," he said. "You're not what I expected."

She pushed her still-damp hair to one side. "What did you expect?" she asked, unable to deny her curiosity.

He shrugged. "Another crazy actress. High maintenance, with a temporary wild hair about moving to Montana."

She smiled because what he'd described was a valid cliché. Actresses weren't known for their stability. "This is my home," she said. "Any time I spend away from here is temporary. This is home for me," she repeated.

"I can see that. You're lucky you've found a place," he said and pulled her into his arms. He gently rubbed his forehead against hers, then lowered his mouth to hers and kissed her.

Gwen felt her pulse pick up and her bones soften.

He slid his fingers through her hair and pulled his mouth from hers. He took a quick sharp breath and swore. "Gonna try to be a responsible adult this time. Are you on the Pill?"

Her stomach twisted at his question. "No, but—"

He swore again. "But?"

"But my doctor told me it would probably be hard for me to get pregnant." She remembered how that conversation with her doctor had been one more blow in a devastating series of events.

He nodded, but to her relief didn't ask any other questions. "From now on we'll use protection."

"Okay," she said and leaned into his hard, warm chest. His outer strength was just a representation of his inner strength. She rubbed her hand over his chest up to his shoulder. "Can we get started on *from now on?*"

He immediately pushed open her robe and slid it down her body. "Oh, yeah."

"One more thing," she said, surrendering to the spell he wove over her.

"What?"

"You really could pose for that centerfo—"

He covered her mouth with a kiss. "Shut up," he muttered.

The next three days they fell into a pattern of rising in the morning and taking care of the horses. In the afternoon, Luc conducted business; Gwen did additional work with the horses or went into town. She lived for the evenings. They were better than the best chocolate she'd ever eaten.

She and Luc shared dinner, usually prepared by his chef, sometimes wine and conversation. Sometimes poker, never television, always sex. Gwen couldn't remember being this happy. Ever.

On Wednesday, she returned from the barn, spotting a different SUV in the driveway. The vehicle looked vaguely familiar and she racked her brain. Walking in through the front door, she found Dane Gibson and Luc squaring off against each other. She winced, immediately recalling the charity event she'd agreed to attend with Dane a month ago. At least the event wouldn't take place for a few days.

"Hi," she said when both men turned to look at her.

"Hey, gorgeous," Dane said. "You're looking good."

She couldn't help but smile. Dane was such a poser. He wasn't much of a cowboy, but he did his best to project the image. His primary attraction to her was her celebrity status.

"I see you've met Luc Hudson."

"Of Hudson Pictures," Dane said, clearly impressed. "He was surprised about our date for the annual Montana Charity Event."

She winced again. "I guess it slipped my mind. I apologize. I've had a lot going on."

"That's okay," he said. "We've got two days. I just thought I'd drop in with a bottle of wine so you and I could get reacquainted."

Gwen felt Luc's gaze burning a hole through her. She couldn't resist the urge to move from foot to foot. "Um," she said.

"Yes?" Luc prompted, his expression cool.

She cleared her throat and looked at Dane. "I can't go to the event with you. I'm engaged."

She felt both men staring at her, and she raised her chin.

Dane raised a blond eyebrow. "Kinda fast," he said.

"Yes, it is. Would either of you like some coffee?"

"I'd rather have whiskey," Dane said.

"I'm not thirsty," Luc said.

Great, she thought and headed for the cabinet that held a small stash of liquor. Just great. "I don't keep much around so I can reduce the temptation for Nicki when she visits." She extracted a locked box from the back of the cabinet, performed the combination and pulled out a bottle of whiskey.

Grabbing two shot glasses, she set them on the coffee table along with the bottle. "All yours."

Dane took the bottle and spilled some liquor into a glass. "You have to attend the event," Dane said. "Everyone is counting on you to introduce the keynote speaker. Plus you can plug your horse-rescue program. We had a bargain."

"Bargain?" Luc echoed.

"Dane has agreed to adopt some of my horses after I rehabilitate them."

Luc gave a slow nod. "I could go with you to the benefit," he said.

"Yeah, but that would leave me without a world-class movie star on my arm," Dane countered.

Gwen couldn't resist rolling her eyes. Luc must have caught her because she noticed his lips twitched in amusement. "You don't have a standby?" Luc asked.

"Not like her," Dane said, pointing at Gwen with emphasis. "We don't get a lot of gorgeous movie stars here in Montucky," he added, using a popular nickname for the state.

Luc shrugged. "Will another actress do?"

"Who?" Dane asked, immediately curious.

"She may be too busy, but I could try to pull a few strings. She's in demand now. She's been featured on some magazine covers and had some roles in independent movies."

Dane frowned. "Who is she? Has anyone heard of her?"

"If they haven't heard of her, they will soon enough. I'm not sure you can handle her, though. She's a pistol, a redhead."

Dane puffed up his chest. "I can handle a redhead. Who is it?" he demanded.

"You want to see a photo?"

"Might as well," Dane said with a shrug.

Curious herself, Gwen watched Luc leave the room

and return with his laptop. He pushed a few keys and turned the screen around so that Dane could see a photo of a gorgeous redhead with a killer body wearing a glamorous evening gown.

"She's easy on the eyes."

Gwen immediately recognized the woman and smiled. "Do you really think you can get her? She's very hot right now."

"I can try," Luc said. "Her name is Isabella," he told Dane. "Isabella Hudson."

Dane raised his eyebrows. "Hudson," he said. "I don't suppose there's any relation?"

"She's my sister."

"Humph." Dane looked at Isabella's picture again. "If you can bring me Isabella as my date and you and Gwen attend the event, then we have a deal."

Five minutes later, Dane left the house and drove his SUV out of Gwen's driveway. Gwen breathed a sigh of relief.

"I thought you said you weren't involved with anyone," Luc said.

"I'm not," she said. "And I wasn't involved with Dane. He offered some good advice and support when I first started the rescues."

"But he made a run at you," Luc guessed.

"There was one night when he tried—" She broke off, surprised at her sudden feelings of self-consciousness. "Dane's the kind of man who makes a run at every woman. He'll make a run at Isabella, so you need to decide how you feel about that."

"Isabella grew up with three brothers. She can handle

herself." He chuckled. "Ol' Dane must have been disappointed. He took that bottle of wine with him."

"He's probably already on the phone with some
gossipy social columnist, spreading the news that he has
bagged three celebrities for his big party."

"But he didn't get you," Luc said, pulling her
against him.

"He didn't really want me. He wanted Gwen
McCord, movie star."

"Then he's a fool," Luc said and took her mouth in
a kiss.

Although she wouldn't admit it to anyone, Gwen
cherished the following days. Since turning the guest
bedroom into an office, Luc took care of business during
the day and burned down her bed every night. It wasn't
all sex, though. He helped her with the horses, played
poker with her and put together a Web site for the horse-
rescue program. He even mapped out a business plan to
help her with the organization of volunteers and financial planning and a tentative plan for the summer camp
she wanted to start.

Gwen had been too involved with the everyday needs
of the horses to think about the business end of things,
but she knew she couldn't rely on her income and her
uncle's generosity forever to subsidize the program.

Isabella had agreed to attend the charity event with
Dane on the condition that she and Gwen enjoy a day
at a spa on the day of the gala.

Gwen and Luc traveled to the Bitterroot Valley area
where Dane's grand party would take place. They went

to the airport to pick up Luc's sister, who was arriving via private jet.

From inside the small terminal, Gwen watched as Luc's sister, her red hair flying in the wind, descended the stairs with an animal clutched to her breast. Her faux-fur coat flapped open, and Gwen immediately felt a shot of pity for the young woman.

"She's got to be freezing," Gwen said.

"I warned her," Luc replied. "And I warned you. Bella is—" he paused and smiled "—a force of nature."

Bella burst inside the terminal, her mouth forming a perfect O. "What in the world would possess anyone to live in this climate? Are you sure Montana isn't a glacier in disguise?"

"Good to see you, too," Luc said, taking his beautiful sister into his arms. "I told you it was colder than freezing. Bitter cold."

"B-b-but, this is ridiculous," she said, looking over his shoulder, her blue-eyed gaze meeting Gwen's. Her lips immediately formed a dazzling smile. "Gwen McCord, it's you."

The dog she carried gave a little yip. "You're mashing Muffin, Luc."

"One can only hope," he muttered, releasing his sister. "Bella, this is Gwen."

Bella threw him a quick scowl before she turned to Gwen. "I'm delighted to meet you. I've admired your work."

"Thank you," Gwen said, her gaze drawn to the animal in her arms as she tried to determine the breed of Muffin. The dog appeared to be a mixture of shih tzu and terrier. Bulldog? It was so ugly it was almost cute.

"What possessed you to move here? Tell me it's temporary," Bella said.

Gwen shook her head. "I love what I'm doing here. I wouldn't trade it for an Oscar."

"Wow," Bella said, her face solemn. She shook her head as if she couldn't comprehend it. "Well, let's talk about it while we're at the spa." She turned to Luc. "Do you want some pics at the spa for PR?"

"Good idea," Luc said and glanced at Gwen. "Are you okay with that?"

"As long as I'm dressed," she said, amazed at how their minds worked in tandem.

Bella waved her hand. "Oh, don't worry. We'll just let them take photos while we're getting pedicures."

"I'll be wearing closed-toe heels, but—"

"If you've been stuck on a ranch, then I'm sure your feet will appreciate a little pampering."

Hours later, after a facial and a massage, Gwen sat next to Bella as a photographer took photos of them getting pedicures. "I can't lie," Gwen said. "I've missed this."

"I always say pedicures should be mandatory for women. Tax deductible. Insurance should cover them."

Gwen smiled. "Sounds like a good idea. I saw you in the film *Non-Tranquil*. You were very good."

"Oh, thank you. If only Spielberg would notice," Bella said.

"He will," Gwen said. "You're talented and beautiful and you have the fire."

"I just hope I'm not old and gray by the time I get a lead part. Sometimes being a member of the Hudson family doesn't work in my favor."

"You have to be twice as good as other people," Gwen said. "Luckily for you, that isn't difficult."

Bella met her gaze. "You're right and thank you for the vote of confidence. I can see why my brother is attracted to you."

Gwen glanced at the photographer. "Did you get enough?"

The woman nodded. "Yes. I'll e-mail the photos to Mr. Hudson."

Gwen thanked the woman and turned to Bella. "It's nice of you to agree to attend this charity event on such short notice."

Bella gave a little snort. "Luc reminded me that I owed him a favor. Oh, who am I fooling? I would do just about anything for him. He promotes me any chance he gets. I'm very lucky." She paused a half beat. "The woman who gets him will be very lucky, too."

"I wouldn't think he would be the type to settle down," Gwen ventured.

"That's where you're wrong. He has this playboy image, but he's incredibly perceptive, very intuitive. Once he commits himself, he's in all the way. He's been a problem solver since he was born. He needs someone who appreciates those qualities and who doesn't take advantage of him."

Gwen nodded. "We live in very different worlds."

"I noticed the way you look at him, the way he

touches you." Bella met her gaze. "Different worlds haven't stopped you two from becoming lovers."

"We're engaged," she said, unsure of how much Bella knew. "Of course we're passionate about each other."

Bella gave her a searching glance and lowered her voice. "Real passion wasn't part of the plan, though, was it? One warning—don't lie to him. Don't keep secrets from him. You'll live to regret it."

Eight

Luc couldn't keep his eyes off Gwen as they entered the ball. She gave her wrap to the woman in the coatroom and pushed her golden hair behind her shoulder. Her black velvet dress skimmed over her creamy shoulders, dipped low to reveal a hint of her delicious cleavage and hugged her curves like a lover. Her lips were crimson, her eyes dramatic; she looked like the definition of the term *heartbreaker*.

It was as if she'd adapted a different persona. Perhaps she had. Every head turned as she walked through the entrance of the ballroom.

"You look beautiful," he whispered in her ear. "But you also look damn good naked in a barn."

Her lips tilted in a secret smile. She met his gaze and

stood on tiptoe to press her lips against his. "You just said something perfect."

Cameras flashed, but Luc just drew her closer, his fingers enjoying the sensation of velvet over her waist and hips. The moment was magical.

"I can't believe it," Bella said, interrupting Luc as she nodded to the left. "Look who's here."

Reluctantly pulling his gaze from Gwen, Luc caught sight of the woman Bella was referring to and shook his head. "Leslie Shay."

"Who is it?" Gwen asked.

"Paparazzi. She lives to dig the dirt on Hudsons," he said.

"What I want to know is when does it cross the line to stalker?" Bella asked.

"Unfortunately, when it's the press, that line is pretty muddy," Luc said.

"I'll say," Gwen said and slid her hand under Luc's chin. "Let's give her something to talk about." She pulled his head down and kissed him full on the mouth.

He heard a roar of applause and peripherally noticed the flash of cameras. He pulled back slightly and laughed. "You know how to work the room without moving from one spot."

"I'm just like you," Gwen confided. "Fifteen minutes and I'm done."

"Then we'd better get moving. Let's face the bearded dragon first." He led her toward Leslie Shay.

Leslie immediately motioned for her cameraman. "Luc Hudson and Gwen McCord, you pulled a fast one on us. We never saw you two as a couple until you announced your engagement. How did you manage to keep your relationship secret?"

"Montana is very cold," Gwen said with a smile. "It discourages the paparazzi, who are accustomed to the warm weather in L.A."

"It's ironic that your engagement coincides with your sister Nicki's visit to rehab, Gwen. Care to comment on that?" Leslie asked.

Watching Gwen's face turn pale, Luc stepped forward. "Gwen is naturally very concerned about her sister. We both are. Nicki has experienced some deep pain in her life, and she hasn't always handled it well. We're both proud of her for getting the help she needs."

"Still, this can't be convenient for Hudson Pictures with the summer release on the horizon," Leslie said.

"I can tell you're a sensitive woman," Gwen said. "I so appreciate your interest in my sister. She's very dear to me. More than anything, I want her healthy and happy."

Leslie nodded. "Always a class act, Gwen. Is there any chance we'll be seeing you in a project with Hudson Pictures soon?"

Gwen laughed. "I'm retired and engaged."

"A loss for the rest of us," Leslie said. "I can't help but believe your ex-husband isn't kicking himself up and down the street. He hasn't had a true hit since your last film."

Luc stepped in again. "Sorry, Leslie, they're motioning for my fiancée. Enjoy the party," he said and guided Gwen away.

With his arm around her, he felt her take a deep breath. "You okay?"

She nodded. "She's a regular badger, isn't she?"

"And then some. I think she had a crush on my uncle that never panned out. Unrequited passion, or something like that."

"Maybe it's good that we're making this appearance tonight. Prep for L.A." She gave a cryptic smile. "The same way kindergarten is prep for medical school. This is looking like a long night."

"Afterward you get a hot tub," he said. "And me."

Her lips curved in a sensual grin. "That's motivating."

Gwen and Luc made the rounds, and when it came time to introduce the keynote speaker, Gwen captured and held the attention of everyone in the room. She spoke with such passion and conviction that even Luc felt himself holding his breath.

Bella touched his shoulder. "She's amazing. Are you sure you can't talk her into coming back into the business?"

As Gwen finished, he watched her walk down the stairs and saw a flicker of vulnerability cross her face. "Not now."

Throughout the evening, people approached Gwen and Bella and asked for their autographs and to have pictures taken with them.

Luc pulled her away. "How's it going?"

"I'm about done," Gwen said. "Even though it's a friendly crowd, it's wearing and I'm out of practice."

"Could have fooled me," Luc said. "I'm all for saying our goodbyes."

Luc shook hands with Dane and hugged his sister.

"You owe me," Bella said.

"You're a glutton for attention. You loved every minute of it," he chided.

"Except the freezing temps. She's different," Bella said, nodding toward Gwen. "I mean that in a good way. But not your type, right?"

"Fishing," Luc said. "I know better than to bite."

"Okay, be that way. Love you," she said and hugged him again.

Extracting Gwen from a group of fans, he led her toward the coatroom. Just after he helped her with her coat, a woman approached them.

"Everyone else may be fawning all over you, but I know the truth. You left your husband high and dry after agreeing to do his movie, then welshing on the deal. When he couldn't get the backing he needed for the movie, your husband had to fire a lot of people. My husband was one of those people. You have no idea how many people's lives you ruined with your—"

Refusing to allow this woman to continue to blast Gwen, Luc stepped in front of her. "That's enough. You have no idea what went on between Gwen and her ex-husband. She doesn't deserve your wrath because of Peter Horrigan's poor planning. Excuse us," he said and led Gwen away.

He bundled her into the waiting limo, where she leaned her head back against the seat and sighed. "And this is just the beginning," she said.

Exhausted and raw from the exposure to invasive questions, Gwen entered the suite reserved for her and Luc and headed straight for one of the bedrooms. She immediately began to ditch her jewelry and accessories. She pulled off her earrings and necklace, kicked the designer shoes from her numb feet and reached for the zipper on her dress.

Luc's hands covered hers, provoking a different set of emotions. "I can handle this," he said.

Conflicted, she let him slide the zipper all the way down to the base of her spine. Cool air rushed over her bare skin, but his hands quickly replaced the dress.

"You did very well tonight. Between Leslie Shay and that crazed woman who approached us at the coatroom, I would have expected you to crack, at least a little, but you didn't."

A feeling of suffocation closed over her. Hating that she was being forced to live a lie again, she stepped away from Luc. "I was hoping people wouldn't be asking questions about Peter."

"You had a very public relationship," Luc pointed out.

"Not by my choice," she said, feeling a trickle of bitterness slide through her like acid.

"From the outside looking in, it appeared you enjoyed the attention as much as he did."

"It was novel in the beginning, but very quickly I wanted to keep our relationship more private. Peter didn't agree. He always said it was silly not to use our relationship to further our careers. I think it was more about *his* career." She broke off, remembering the arguments they'd had. "I'm sure I don't have to tell you how different a relationship can be on the inside from how it looks on the outside."

"You haven't talked about your marriage much," he said.

"And I don't want to now," she said. "I think I could use a good night's sleep."

"Your bath is waiting," he said with an unreadable expression on his face.

She blinked in surprise. "How did that happen?"

"I called ahead."

Gwen's conflicting feelings swelled inside her again. On one hand, she deeply resented that Luc had been the one to put her in the position of leading a public lie. On the other hand, she couldn't help feeling protected when he sprang to her defense.

"I hate living a lie," she said.

"It's not my favorite thing either," he said.

"How can we be involved? Having an affair in this situation? It's insane. Is it just convenience?"

Luc gave a rough laugh. "I'd say my feelings for you are damn inconvenient. Maybe yours for me are, too. Do you really want to turn your back on them?"

"Yes," she said. "Yes, I do."

He stood there, looking at her, making her feel as if he could read her like a book, making her feel as if he knew the truth about how much she wanted him.

"I do want to turn my back on my feelings for you," she admitted. "But I can't."

After the charity party, Luc and Gwen spent five days in near seclusion and Luc loved every minute of it. He was surprised at how much he liked being away from the insanity of L.A. Both he and Gwen knew, however, that the time was coming when they would need to go to L.A. and make appearances.

Luc conducted a conference call with his father and two brothers, along with his assistant so he wouldn't need to duplicate his efforts. The call lasted until 6:00 p.m. He expected to find Gwen in the kitchen, thawing and reheating a meal his chef had sent, but she was nowhere around.

Pulling on his jacket, hat and gloves, he walked to the barn and found her in a stall with an elderly gelding. She stroked his neck and spoke to him in a soft, sweet voice.

He felt an overwhelming desire for more of her. He wanted more of her sex, more of her laughter, more of her trust. The strength of his passion seemed to ratchet upward with each passing day. At some point it would abate. It had to. Until then, he was determined to have her in every way possible.

Watching her pet the horse for a moment longer, he moved closer to the stall door.

She must have heard his movement because she looked over her shoulder at him. "Hi," she said.

"Hi. Who do we have here?"

Gwen looked up at the black gelding. "Fred. I've spent more Friday and Saturday nights with this guy than any other since I moved to Montana. He was my first rescue, and he'd been so abused that the vet didn't think he would survive. But he did."

"Does he know all your secrets?" Luc asked.

She smiled. "Quite a few. Fred's an excellent listener. No judgment, just nods and snorts every now and then." She met Luc's gaze. "We have to go to L.A. soon, don't we?"

Hearing the note of dread in her voice, he nodded and entered the stall. "What are you afraid of?"

She bit her lip. "Being asked questions I don't want to answer."

"That's easy," he said. "You just practice a prepared response and change the subject to what you want to promote."

She watched him silently as if she didn't believe him.

"You're worried about questions about your ex-husband and your marriage."

"They keep digging. No matter what I tell them, they keep digging."

He heard an undercurrent of pain, and his instincts went on alert. "Is there something I should know?"

"No," she said quickly and turned away from him.

She was hiding something. "You should tell me," he said. "It's always better to be prepared."

"It's not that easy," she said. "And it's not something I discuss with anyone."

He inclined his head toward the horse. "Including Fred?"

"Fred won't tell," she said, her lips twitching slightly. "And he always takes my side."

He walked to her and pulled her against him. "Thank goodness Fred can't do everything. You'll enjoy this trip to L.A. Shopping, massages, spa rituals, all that girl stuff. Good food and most importantly…"

"The press junket," she said miserably.

"No," he said. "Me."

She smiled. "Are all the Hudsons as insufferably secure as you are?"

"It helps when you're born into the family," he said, guiding her out of the stall. "You understand your place and purpose."

"And yours is?"

"Problem solver," he said.

She stopped, raising her hand to his jaw. "Mr. Fix-it," she said. "Do you ever want to take a break from it?"

"I've done that here," he said. "For the first time in what feels like forever."

"But you haven't taken a break," she said. "You rescued Pyrrha twice, and you've made appearances."

"It didn't feel the same," he said, still figuring out what that meant for him.

"So maybe you're not Mr. L.A. after all," she teased.

"We'll see," he said. "You and I have one more night in no man's land. Then it's off to the 'City of Angels' and massages and great food. Tell me what you miss about the hood and I'll make sure we hit everything."

The following afternoon, they left for the airport and flew via private jet to L.A. Gwen had to admit that flying on a private jet was so civilized compared with commercial air travel. She sat across from Luc and ate fresh fruit and sandwiches. Chocolate truffles were waiting.

Luc worked on his laptop computer and chugged mineral water. "Our first appearance is two days from now," he said, narrowing his eyes at the screen. "Charity for homelessness. Then the next day we've been asked to appear on a morning show."

"If we're not appearing for two days, why did we leave so early?"

He looked up from his computer. "So you can do a little shopping, get a massage and hopefully we can work in something else."

"What?" she asked and ate another grape.

"I'll tell you if I can make it happen."

"What is it?" she demanded.

He shook his head. "I don't want you to be disappointed. If I can pull it off, it will happen tonight."

Gwen glanced down at her jeans, boots and sweater. "Should I be dressed differently?"

He shook his head again. "You're dressed perfectly for this. When we land, be prepared for a shell game."

She shook her head. "Oh, my. Luc Hudson, man of intrigue."

He shot her a mocking look of threat. "This once, just trust me. If this works out, you'll be pleased."

"Now you've got me dying of curiosity."

"Eat some chocolate."

She ate several chocolates. After they landed at the private terminal, Luc told her to remain seated, and she watched the airline attendant and copilot get into a limo.

"Nice ride," she murmured, watching as a hybrid vehicle approached the jet. "Who is riding in that?"

Luc shot her a mysterious grin. "We are."

Before they descended the steps, Luc donned a pilot's cap and the jet lights were dimmed. "Careful on the steps," he said.

"A masquerade," she said.

"Not totally," he said. "I'm licensed to fly, but the car is borrowed. I don't want it traced to either you or me."

"Good grief," she said as he helped her into the small

car. Seconds later, he climbed in and pushed the driver's seat back to allow him to stretch his legs. "Are you sure you haven't ever worked for the CIA or FBI?"

"The CIA and FBI could take lessons from Hudson Pictures. Relax. This is going to take a while," he said.

An hour and a half later, after a circuitous route through a residential Beverly Hills neighborhood, a drive down the freeway and another windy ride that seemed to backtrack, Luc pulled into a gated facility.

"New Beginnings," she said, reading the sign. "Nicki is here. I get to see her!"

He gave his identification to security and nodded. "For a few minutes."

Her heart squeezed tight in her chest. "Oh, Luc, I can't tell you how much this means to me. I thought you said they wanted to keep the patients away from everyone, including family."

"They do for the first week or so. She's doing well, and her physicians agreed that a visit from you wouldn't hurt her progress. In fact, they thought it would help. But for her protection and Hudson Pictures', we didn't want to publicize your visit."

She nodded, amazed at the measures Luc had taken to make this happen. "I don't know what to say. Thank you just isn't enough."

Luc pulled up to a side door of a building. "Go see your sister," he said. "She's waiting for you."

Gwen's eyes burned with tears, and she wrapped her arms around him. "Thank you," she whispered and reveled in his strength for a moment before she got out of the car.

A male attendant was waiting at the door to allow her

inside. "Miss McCord," he said. "Your sister is waiting down the hall to the left."

Anticipation growing inside her, she walked quickly down the hallway. Turning the corner, she looked into a parlor and saw Nicki sitting in a chair with her hands folded in her lap. Her blonde hair tied back in a ponytail, her face scrubbed free of makeup, Nicki looked like the little sister Gwen remembered from years gone by.

"Nicki," she whispered.

Her sister's head turned and Nicki met her gaze. Her expression was at first cautious, but when Gwen approached her with open arms, Nicki jumped up to meet her.

Nicki flew into her arms and burst into tears. "Gwen, I'm so sorry. I've made such a mess of things. I should have listened to you. Do you realize I almost k-k-killed that family—" Her voice broke and she sobbed.

"Hush," Gwen said, cradling her sister. "The important thing is you realize you got offtrack and you're getting the help you need."

Pulling back, Nicki looked up at Gwen, her expression full of guilt. "And I'm so sorry you had to be dragged into this."

"It's just for a few weeks," Gwen told her. "If that's what it takes for you to find your way again, it's a small sacrifice."

"But I know how much you hate L.A.," Nicki said, sniffling.

"But I'll eat well," Gwen said.

Nicki gave a shaky laugh. "You always try to find the good in the bad."

"Survival skill," Gwen said.

"Luc Hudson's a tough one," Nicki said. "But you know, he was so protective of me when all this happened. I was stunned. Before that, I could feel his impatience every time there was a memo from his assistant. But when I did this incredibly stupid thing, he was there and he got me where I needed to be. He was compassionate. I would never have expected that. I hear he's tough with the actors and wields a glove of velvet steel with the press. I believe it now. Has he been a total pain in the ass?"

Gwen blinked. "Uh, no. He actually helped rescue a mare. He's a horseman. Who knew?"

Nicki searched Gwen's face. "You're sure? You're not lying? I don't want you to take any abuse on my account."

"Not if you count meals flown in from his chef and chocolate on the private flight to L.A.," Gwen said with a smile.

Nicki chuckled. "So you've been in heaven," she said.

"I wouldn't say that," Gwen said and took Nicki's hand. "We don't have much time. Tell me what's going on with you."

"I'm learning to be my own mom," Nicki said sheepishly.

"Oh, you'll be a great mom. And what a great daughter you have."

"I'm so lucky I have you in my life," Nicki said. "So lucky."

"I feel the same way," Gwen replied.

"I'm going to be better when I get out of here," Nicki said.

"You already are," Gwen said and hugged her sister again.

An hour later, she slid into the seat beside Luc. "You have officially become the superhero for the McCord women."

He gave a noncommittal glance. "How is she?"

"Great. I can already tell this is exactly what she needed. I'm so grateful that you took her here. She is too."

"Over the next two weeks, hold that thought," he said grimly.

Gwen nodded. "It's worth it. Anything is worth Nicki getting better."

"Are you ready for the roller-coaster ride?"

"Probably not, but I'll do what needs to be done," she said, starting to come down after the high of seeing her sister.

"We're staying at the family beach house tonight," he said. "I thought you would enjoy the morning view. As far as the press is concerned, we're at my bungalow."

"When does the insanity start?"

"The day after tomorrow."

"You're pretty amazing," she said, feeling the walls around her heart begin to crumble.

Moments later Luc drove through another security gate and up a winding road to a two-story cottage, where the lights and a middle-aged man dressed in denim welcomed them.

"Good evening, Mr. Hudson," the man said and nodded toward her. "Good evening, ma'am."

"This is Wilfred, but he goes by Fred. He's been with the family since before I was born. Fred, this is Gwen McCord."

"Pleasure to meet you, Miss McCord," Fred said,

pulling their luggage from the back of the car. "You're more beautiful in person than your photos, if you don't mind my saying so."

"Fred's a flirt," Luc muttered.

"Thank you very much, Fred. You're too kind. I'm partial to Freds," Gwen said, shooting Luc a sideways glance.

"Is that so?" Fred said, swaggering a bit as he led them inside the cottage. "All that airbrushed hogwash. There's nothing like the real thing. Real skin. Real beauty. And that's what you've got. Now where should I take the luggage?"

"To my room," Luc said. "My fiancée will be staying with me."

Gwen blinked at his possessive tone.

"You finally found one worth keeping," Fred said. "My congratulations." He offered his hand to Luc and shook his hand, then turned to Gwen. "I believe it's customary to give the bride best wishes." He took Gwen's hand and lifted it to his lips. "In this case you may need them," he muttered.

Gwen laughed.

Luc scowled. "If anyone except you had said that—"

"Off with the head," Fred finished for him. "Truthfully," he said to Gwen. "He's a good man."

Gwen stood silently for a moment and nodded. "I know."

The three climbed the stairs to a beautiful master suite that awaited with a bottle of champagne and flowers. Gwen walked to the shuttered front window and stared out at the sea below, white crests beating against the shore. She inhaled, wanting to smell the salty scent.

As if he sensed it, Luc cracked the window and she inhaled again. "It's delicious," she said, closing her eyes for a second. "I haven't been back in over a year and I still love Montana best, but the ocean is a close second."

"Speaking of delicious," he said, and she felt the cool glass lifted to her lips. She opened her mouth and allowed the bubbly champagne to slide down her throat.

"This is too wonderful," she whispered, knowing she was treading on dangerous ground. Being with Luc was so marvelous she never wanted it to end, but she knew it had to end sometime.

Not tonight, though, she told herself as she raised her mouth to his. Not tonight.

Nine

The hint of sunlight streaming through the blinds awakened Gwen the next morning. Yawning, she stretched and looked at Luc, asleep next to her. His dark eyelashes contrasted with his tanned skin. A sexy shadow of a beard covered his jaw and strong chin. Against the hard planes of his face, his mouth stood out in sensual relief.

Her heart raced and her blood heated. She looked away, her reaction making her feel like a crazy woman. Maybe she was crazy. Their situation sure was.

She'd been certain Luc was like her ex-husband—power hungry, manipulative, ruthless when necessary. She took another glance at him. The truth was he could be ruthless when necessary, but he wasn't power hungry.

He was strong inside and out. He managed the press, but he had flat-out told her what she had to do.

Somehow she felt both challenged and protected by him. If their lives were different, if he weren't firmly entrenched in L.A.'s culture and she weren't firmly committed to her life in Montana, she wondered if he could have been the one for her.

Whoa.

She needed a shower or a brisk walk. Or both. Gently rolling to the edge of the bed, she pushed one foot out from the covers.

A strong hand clamped around the ankle still underneath. "Where do you think you're going?" he asked in a sleep-husky voice.

She glanced back at him, her heart turning over at the sight of his bare chest and sexy blue eyes. "Walk on the beach," she said. "It will feel like a heat wave compared with Montana."

"Good idea. Let me pull on some clothes and I'll join you."

So much for a brisk walk to clear her head, but she couldn't muster a complaint when they walked down the path to the beach and he took her hand. With his fingers linked through hers, the sun shining through the L.A. haze and the waves beating against the shore, Gwen felt an overwhelming sense of contentment.

"Admit it," he said, "you've missed it."

"The ocean," she conceded. "There's something about the rhythm of the waves and the warmth of the sun. The only two things that would make it better would be if it were warm enough to go barefoot and…"

"And?"

"And I bet June would love the ocean."

He tapped her nose with his forefinger and grinned. "I bet she would." He squinted toward the sky. "Come to think of it, I can't remember the last time I took a walk on the beach."

"You're usually running, listening to music or a book on your iPod."

He tossed her a sideways glance. "How did you know?"

"Type A all the way," she said.

He slid his hand around her waist and gently pinched her ribs. "You're no slouch. You go from being an Academy Award–nominated actress to living in the sticks and rescuing horses. You get up at the crack of dawn every morning, and I didn't see you taking any voluntary downtime," he said, drawing her against him. "Except when I seduced you, which I'd like to do right now."

As he took her mouth, it occurred to her that he made her forget her surroundings so much that she wondered if he could take her anywhere. Scandalized by the thought, she drew back and shook her head. "That's a little more than I want to give the gossip magazines."

He made a sound between a sigh and a groan. "If you hadn't been such a popular actress, then we wouldn't have this problem."

"If I hadn't been well-known, you would have never come to Montana and I wouldn't be here right now," she told him.

He met her gaze with some kind of powerful emotion seeming to rumble beneath the surface of him. "That would have been a damn shame. You know, if you stay around me long enough, you may decide you like L.A. better than you thought you did."

Her stomach clenched because she knew everything between them was temporary. "By the time our masquerade is over, you'll be glad to get rid of me."

"What if I'm not? What if you're not?"

Her heart stuttered and she closed her eyes and shook her head. "I can't go there. You and I are worlds apart."

"Yet we meet in so many ways," he said.

"It's temporary," she said firmly, meeting his gaze.

"We'll see," he said and urged her into a jog.

After a wicked brunch of bacon and pancakes with berries and maple syrup, they left the cottage and Luc dropped her off at a spa. "My assistant made the appointment for you. As far as I'm concerned, you don't need to do a thing, but she was appalled that I would start you on a PR tour without allowing you to get a massage and whatever else you women like to get."

"She was correct. Please tell her I said thank you."

"I will. A driver will pick you up in two hours to take you to Rodeo Drive. Buy whatever you want and put it on my card," he said, giving her his credit card.

"Are you sure you want to do this? I could do serious damage to this card on Rodeo Drive."

"Go right ahead. You'll need some cocktail gowns for some of the evening affairs. Get at least three or four," he told her. "My assistant has our itinerary, but as you know, it's subject to change. Let me key her number into your cell," he said. "And mine," he added. "And your driver." He glanced up. "You look overwhelmed."

"I'm not," she said but didn't sound very convincing even to herself.

"Okay, then don't try to get everything this afternoon. We're eating at The Ivy tonight."

"Showtime begins," she said, recalling that the restaurant was popular for celebrity sightings, therefore popular with the paparazzi.

He nodded. "Then we go back to my bungalow and it's just you and me," he said and brushed his lips over hers.

Taking a deep breath, she girded herself for the job she'd accepted in exchange for her sister's health and future and got out of the car. As soon as she stepped through the door, she was ushered to a private room and given a massage. Afterward, she sipped green tea until a gorgeous Latino man walked through the door and put his hands on his hips as he stared at her. "You are a disaster," Carlos said.

Gwen's heart lifted at the sight of her favorite former stylist, and she rose to embrace him. "I live to give you a challenge," she joked. "When did you start working here? I thought your salon was in a different location."

"I'm a man of many places now, Gwen, darling," he said, taking her by the hand to the hair styling room and guiding her to a chair. "Four in California, and I'm launching in New York City in six months."

She gave a mock gasp. "You've become a chain."

He gave a real gasp. "Never." He raised his hands. "Everyone needs me, so I try to find a way to accommodate. Now let's look at this mess on your head that others would call hair. You want to go darker or platinum?"

"I like the color," she said. "And since you haven't

set up a location in Montana, I don't want to have to deal with roots. I think the local market carries hair coloring, though."

Carlos gasped again. "Over-the-counter hair color? You wouldn't dare. Now that you're back in town, why do you worry about touch-ups?"

"I'm not totally back in town," she said.

"But aren't you engaged to one of the Hudsons?" he mused, sifting his fingers through her hair. "Or is that just for show?"

"Oh, no," she said, panic slicing through her. She flashed her ring. "It's not for show, but we'll be splitting our time between Montana and here. Besides, Luc *likes* my hair color," she said, even though she had no idea what Luc's preference was.

Carlos heaved a sigh. "Okay, just a few highlights here and there and a glossing." He made a face. "You definitely need a cut. What *is* this style?"

"It's called put it in a ponytail when you wake up and go out to the barn."

"Barn." He muttered something in Spanish. "We'll have you looking like the head turner I know you are in no time."

Gwen allowed Carlos to work his magic, but she wasn't all that crazy about being the head turner he wanted her to be. In fact, after she left the salon, the first thing she bought was a baseball cap, which she pulled over her freshly styled hair. If Carlos had known, he would have had her head.

With sunglasses planted firmly on her nose, she made her way through several stores to find appropriate costumes, er, clothing for her role as Luc's fiancée. What would Luc's fiancée wear? Flashy designer clothing. She would be attention-getting, while Gwen was not.

Compromising, she allowed a kind salesclerk to help her select some flattering but less attention-grabbing clothes than she would have chosen in her past life with Peter. When the salesclerk realized who Gwen was, she was starstruck and asked for an autograph. Gwen complied and managed to exit without causing a fuss.

Like magic, her driver appeared, this time with Luc sitting in the backseat. Finishing a cell phone conversation, he looked at her and smiled. "Like the cap," he said with a half grin.

She wrinkled her nose. "I decided to ease into this. I didn't want people recognizing me. I always underestimate that." She pulled off her cap.

"My God," Luc said, gaping at her hair. "What did they do to you?"

"Added a few highlights," Gwen said uncertainly. "He mentioned going darker or platinum."

"Thank goodness you didn't let him do either of those. Who was this quack, anyway?"

She chuckled. "Only the most popular hairstylist in L.A. Maybe the entire country."

Luc sighed. "The cut's okay. But I think your natural color is the best."

She couldn't stop herself from smiling. "Thank you. I told him you liked my natural color to keep him from doing something drastic."

"You were right."

"Do you hate it?"

"No," he said. "You would be beautiful bald."

She inhaled sharply, then leaned toward him and pressed her mouth to his. "This is a crazy situation, and I do hate it. But when I'm with you, it just doesn't seem so bad."

"Hold that thought," he said, taking her mouth and kissing her thoroughly. "Hold that thought every time you feel a doubt coming on."

It seemed only seconds passed before the driver pulled in front of The Ivy Restaurant. Gwen combed her fingers through her hair.

Luc framed her face with his hands and kissed her. "Don't think about the crowds or the paparazzi. It's just you and me, okay?"

She took a deep breath and smiled. "Okay."

Luc escorted her from the car and held her close while cameras flashed. She instinctively buried her face against his chest.

"Mr. Hudson, have you and Gwen set the date?" a voice asked.

"Gwen, tell us you're going to make another movie," another said.

"How is Nicki doing?"

Gwen snapped out of her fog and looked into the crowd. "She's doing well. Working hard to be the person she wants to be. I'm so proud of her."

It seemed a thousand cameras flashed.

"I'd like to enjoy dinner with my fiancée, if that's okay with you," Luc said in a long-suffering tone

A collection of chuckles followed. "Hey, you're marrying the sexiest woman alive. What do you expect?"

He tossed them a commanding look. "You think I

don't know that?" he asked and led her inside the restaurant. "Round one," he said to her. "Thank God that's over. Are you okay?"

As long as he put his arm around her, she thought, and nodded. "Yeah, I'm okay."

Even though they were seated at a corner table, several people stopped to greet them. Three male box-office stars offered their congratulations and boldly hinted that they would love to pair up with Gwen in a movie.

Sipping sparkling water with lots of lime, Gwen smiled and demurred each time.

"No wine?" Luc asked.

"I don't drink during PR tours," she said, taking another sip. "I don't want to say anything I'll regret."

Luc made a sound of frustration. "You really are a dream actress. Do you know how many people I have to beg to lay off the sauce?"

"The paparazzi are ruthless. I need all my brain cells."

He chuckled and slid his hand beneath her hair. "You're that rare combination of—"

"A pain in the ass and…" she interjected.

He laughed and shook his head. "Of beauty and sensibility. How stupid was Peter Horrigan?"

She abruptly lost her sense of humor. "He had a different agenda than I did."

Luc nodded and brushed his hand against her cheek. "You look so sad. You have regrets."

"Just one," she said. "But I'm dealing with it."

"Still?"

"Forever," she said and took another sip of her sparkling water. "But that's enough of that discussion."

"Okay. Do you want dessert, or are you ready to go home?"

She smiled. "I can't have dessert at home?"

He gave a wicked chuckle and signaled for the server. "Check, please."

Minutes later, the driver appeared, as he was well paid to do. Luc ushered Gwen into the backseat.

"Thank God that's over," they both said at the same time.

Gwen laughed and so did he; then he pulled her face to his and took her mouth. He could not get enough of her. Everything she did, every move she made, made him want more.

Sliding his tongue inside her sweet mouth, he cradled her face and felt the burn in his gut spread to his groin. She'd made him hard all evening with her tempting smiles and green eyes full of secrets he wanted to learn.

"I can't wait to take you again," he said. "I can't wait to take you in my bed. I've been thinking about it since the first time I saw you."

"Hold me," she said. "Make me forget the craziness."

He stretched his arms around her and clasped her to him. He couldn't get close enough. Taking her mouth in an endless French kiss, he slid his hand beneath her top and touched her skin.

"Another good thing about L.A. is that you don't need to wear as many clothes."

He felt her lips tilt upward against his. "How efficient of you to point that out."

The driver stopped just outside his bungalow. "Thank goodness," Luc said, pulling her from the car.

"See you tomorrow, Lance," he said to the driver. "Thanks. Good night."

"Thank you," Gwen said.

Luc led her through the front door and couldn't wait a second longer. He pulled her against him, cupping her derierre with his hands.

She moaned against his mouth, taking his tongue inside her. He tugged at her clothes, impatient to get closer. He wanted her bare skin against his. He pushed away her shirt. She pushed away his.

He shoved her panties and jeans down her legs. She fumbled with the fastenings to his jeans and plunged her hands inside his underwear.

Luc nearly exploded.

He craved her touch, but if she didn't stop…

He slid his hand between her legs and found her wet and soft. She stopped. He nearly begged her to continue but was determined to feel her completion. He rubbed his thumb over her and she gasped in pleasure.

The sexy sound drove him on. He slid a finger inside her and continued stroking her. Her breathlessness made him as hard as a brick, but he wanted all of her in his hands, in his mouth, in every way possible.

Taking her mouth in a soulful kiss, he continued to play her until she shuddered in pleasure, her climax coming in fits and starts.

"Ohh," she said and plunged her hands into his crotch.

"I don't know how long I can take this," he warned her.

"Fair is fair. Look what you did to me."

Luc made an instantaneous decision driven by primitive need. Grabbing protection from his jeans pocket, he put it on and spun her around, against the wall. Lifting her legs up over his hips, he pulled her down over his swollen masculinity, inch by excruciating inch.

He moaned.

She gasped.

Squeezing her bottom, he began to pump and she flexed. With each thrust, he went deeper. He gazed into her green eyes and felt as if he were under the spell of a lifetime. And he had no desire to break it. He wanted Gwen and nothing else mattered.

Ten

As Gwen awakened the next morning, she sighed, feeling as if she'd contracted some kind of sleeping sickness. Although she wouldn't say it aloud, it was nice knowing she didn't have to be the one up at the crack of dawn to check on her horses. Stretching, she glanced over at Luc's side of the bed, surprised to see it empty.

That gave her a jolt. She was always up early. What was turning her into such a sleeper? Was it the fantastic sex?

Swiping her hair from her face, she rose from bed and pushed her arms into the sleeves of a too-large but very comfy plush terry robe draped over a chair. She tied it around her, went into the bathroom and splashed her face and brushed her teeth, then wandered down the hallway.

She heard Luc before she saw him.

"I'll be in the office within thirty minutes," he said. "I'll have something for the Jake Stratton situation by the time I get in. We just need a sympathetic angle on the guy. Everyone has a sympathetic angle. If not, we'll give him one."

She rounded the corner and saw him pacing in the den, a large window providing a backdrop against his imposing frame. He wore a white shirt with a dark jacket and pants.

Luc chuckled. "You flatter me. It's true I could find a sympathetic angle for a serial killer, but I'm not sure I could sustain it if he keeps murdering innocent people. See you in a bit." He glanced up and his eyes lit up. "Hey, sleepyhead."

"I know," she said. "It's embarrassing. I never sleep in while I'm in Montana."

He shrugged and walked toward her. "Here's your chance. You can go back to bed if you want. I have to go to the office."

"I heard," she said. "You have to produce spin for a serial murderer."

"Not quite," he said with a chuckle and sifted his fingers through her hair. "Crazy, but I like your hair every color you've worn it."

Her heart fluttered. "Thank you," she said. "Do I have an assignment today?"

"Relax. Take a dip in the heated pool. Read something useless. If you need to do more shopping, just call the driver and he'll take you."

She felt a yawn of longing for him and he hadn't even left yet. Stupid. "Did anyone ever tell you how hot you look in California business casual?"

He kissed her and pulled back with more than a hint of reluctance. "No one who counted. Stop tempting me."

"Who me?" she asked. "No makeup, haven't brushed my hair, half-asleep."

"Yeah," he said. "Looks damn good to me." He pushed her away from him. "We've got a charity something tonight. Rest up for it."

"Ah, so I turn into a working girl tonight."

He gave a low growl. "You have no idea what that does to me."

"Give me a hint," she said, playing along.

"Do you know how easy it would be to untie that robe and take you right now?"

The notion made her breathless. "How easy?"

"We'll find out later," he said and gave her another quick kiss. "Call me if you need anything."

Watching him leave, she immediately felt forlorn. Followed quickly by… stupid. Rolling her eyes at herself, she wandered around the bungalow, taking in the sleek, spare decor. Luc allowed no clutter in his home. One more bit of proof that she didn't belong in his life long-term.

Her stomach growled, so she looked in his cabinets for something to eat. Carbs, she thought, wishing for a bagel. Thank goodness she hadn't bought anything that was skintight yesterday. Digging through a cabinet that looked promising, she hit paydirt. Honey wheat bagels. Oh, yes.

She popped one in the toaster and wondered how her horses were doing. She drummed her fingers on the granite counter. Hearing the distant ring of her cell phone, she ran to the bedroom and finally located her purse. The phone stopped ringing.

Scowling, she picked it up to review the missed call. Luc. She hit redial and he immediately answered.

"Hello. Missing your ponies?"

His voice felt like a sensual purr over her nerve endings. "How did you know?"

"Lucky guess," he said. "There's a laptop in the room two doors down from the dining room on the left."

Gwen followed his directions to a large, beautiful office with a huge window and the latest electronics. Glancing around the room, she spotted a laptop on the contemporary desk. "Yes," she said, moving in front of the screen.

"Move the mouse around," he instructed and she did.

Up popped a screen featuring video feed of Pyrrha and Fred. Gwen gasped. "How did you do this?"

"Through your computer at home. It was simple. How's our girl?"

"She looks fine," Gwen said, studying the mare. "Great. Moving around a little. She's so sweet. Afraid to trust but wants to try. I don't know what to say."

"You don't have to say anything. Anytime you want to see your horses, you can. Just go to this live feed, and you can know that they're safe and comfortable."

A lump grew in her throat. "This was really great of you. Amazing. I don't know how to thank you."

"You're creative," he said in a suggestive voice. "I'm sure you'll think of something."

She couldn't hold back a smile. "You're a wicked, wicked man."

"Yeah," he said.

"Yeah," she echoed. "Thank goodness."

He chuckled and the sound seemed to reverberate throughout her. She felt him in her pores, her muscles, blood and bones, and he wasn't even with her.

"Don't get addicted to the screen," he told her. "Take some time off. You'll earn your free time tonight."

"Okay. Thanks," she said and disconnected the call. She stared at the screen until she heard the pop of the toaster. After eating her bagel, she watched the horses a while longer, then wandered through the rest of the bungalow.

She found a media room with a gigantic screen television, a pool table on one side and a poker table on the other. She could easily imagine Luc talking trash and playing with his friends or brothers. Spotting a picture sticking out of a trash can, she picked it up and looked at it.

It was a framed magazine article featuring several photos of Luc, who was described as one of L.A.'s hottest bachelors. In the largest photo, he wore an unbuttoned white shirt. He stared into the camera with a ghost of a sexy smile tilting his lips. His blue eyes blazed with an I'm-gonna-get-you-and-you're-gonna-like-it expression.

She felt a strange tug in her stomach when she thought about how different their lives were. Years ago, she'd been featured in a similar photo spread, a new favorite face. A little time away from Hollywood had convinced her that she wanted no part of the acting scene.

She was more content in Montana than she'd ever been in California, but she couldn't help wondering, for just a moment, how things might have been if she'd met Luc earlier and she hadn't been married.

"It doesn't matter," she whispered to herself and

shook off her thoughts. Turning the photo over to return it to the trash can, she saw a message inscribed on the back. *Happy 30th Birthday to L.A.'s hottest! Good thing you look like your older, but much hotter brothers. Dev and Max.*

She smiled, easily imagining Luc rolling his eyes at the gift. Funny, for all the differences between Luc and her, she'd put her copy of her feature as the sexiest woman in America in the same place—the trash can.

She lingered in the room for a few extra moments, studying Luc's family photos on the wall. There were a few black-and-white pictures of Luc's grandfather and grandmother on the wall. What a dashing pair they were. Luc's grandmother Lillian was the kind of woman who would capture the attention of an entire room, no matter her age. Her talent and reputation were legendary.

The love between Luc's grandfather and grandmother had been so strong that Gwen wondered how Lillian had carried on after Charles's death. She wandered to a photograph of the whole family, grandparents, parents and children, and the sense of continuity tugged at an empty spot inside her.

Her own family was scattered. She'd known only one grandparent and had been fortunate to maintain a special bond with her aunt and uncle in Montana. What must it be like to have that kind of family connection? The pressures and the paybacks. She'd bet the rewards more than made up for any downside.

Smiling sadly to herself, she took one last look at the photograph of Luc and his family and sealed it in her mind. Some way, someday, she would find a way to create that sense of family for herself. It just wouldn't be now, and it wouldn't be with the Hudsons.

Battling horrendous freeway traffic, Luc finally pulled into his garage and climbed out of his hybrid. Pushing his fingers through his hair, he shook his head. What a day.

He walked inside to find Gwen dressed in a green gown that slid over her body like liquid silk. It took only one glance for his blood pressure to rise and his heart to race.

"You look amazing," he said, walking toward her.

"Thank yourself. You bought the dress for me yesterday," she said with a smile and touched his hair. "Rough day?"

He groaned. "You have no idea."

"Working with the serial killer didn't go as easily as planned?"

He chuckled. "Sometimes I think I need to be a shrink."

"You mean that's not one of your degrees? Psychiatrist?"

"No," he said firmly. "But I think I may have made some headway with my problem actor. I kept trying to find a charity where he wanted to get involved. I finally found something."

"What is it?"

"Cat rescue," he said, still not comprehending it himself.

Gwen shot him a look of disbelief. "You're joking."

He shook his head. "Oh, no. Seems our wild man has a soft spot for cats." He loved the way Gwen was tilting her head as if she couldn't comprehend it, because he'd felt the exact same way. "He had several as a child."

She laughed softly. "It always goes back to what we don't get as a child."

"I guess," he said then paused. "What didn't you get?"

"I got a safe place to live, electricity, plenty of food, a good education. I have no real reason to complain," she said.

"But what did you want that you didn't get?"

Closing her eyes, she inhaled. "I wanted to please my parents. I wanted to feel a part of something bigger than myself. I wanted to feel okay about whatever I chose to do, whether it was high profile or low profile. I wanted my little sister not to feel so lost."

His gut twisted at her confession, and he drew her to him. "That's not too much to ask, Gwen."

"Thanks," she said and opened her eyes. "But you've played shrink enough today. What kind of charity event are we attending tonight?"

He shrugged. "Don't know, although I'm sure it's an extremely worthy one." He pulled out his BlackBerry and punched in a code. "Looks like the American Heart Association." He met her gaze and smiled. "Appropriate," he said. "You'll be breaking hearts tonight left and right."

Thirty minutes later, after Luc took a shower and changed into a tux, the two of them sat in the back of a limo and headed for the charity event. "So, my goal tonight is to find a way to mention *The Waiting Room* in a positive way several times during the night," Gwen reviewed.

"If we can," he said. "If not, then just say something good about Hudson Pictures."

She nodded. "I can do that. Any hot-button subjects?"

"Just your sister. If asked about her, just say how proud you are that she's taking steps to straighten herself out."

"That one isn't very hard, because it's so true," Gwen said. The limo pulled in front of the extravagant hotel and she sighed. "Showtime again."

She waited for Luc to get out of the car to help her. The cameras flashed and she smiled, waving to the crowd of onlookers. A female reporter with a microphone immediately approached Gwen and Luc.

"Good evening. Chelsea Walker with ENTV. Congratulations on your engagement. Any details on the wedding yet?"

"We'll tell you as soon as we have everything finalized," Luc said with a game smile.

The reporter shook her finger doubtfully. "I've heard that line before. On a more serious note, Gwen, how is your sister, Nicki, doing?"

"Very well," Gwen said. "I actually got to see her recently. She's doing some important work on herself. I'm very proud of her. And of course we're also excited about her upcoming movie. It's a breakout role for Nicki in a great action movie. Hudson always puts out great entertainment."

The reporter turned to Luc. "Any chance Hudson will be luring Gwen back to the big screen? Her fans miss her."

"I'm concentrating on luring her down the aisle," Luc said. "We should get inside. Great talking with you, Chelsea," he said and guided Gwen inside.

She laughed to herself. "It never changes," she said. "You get the same questions and give the same answers over and over again."

"Repetition is the key, although we may have to throw them a couple of bones to keep the interest going."

"What kind of bones?" she asked.

He shrugged. "Something about you considering a movie role."

She shook her head vehemently. "Try something else. That will cause me more trouble than it's worth."

"Never say never."

"Never ever to the hundredth power," she said.

"We'll see," he said and guided her into the ballroom.

His lack of acceptance of her unwillingness to get back into the movie world bothered her, but she hoped he was just speaking from a PR standpoint. Either way, she had no intention of spreading that rumor.

She and Luc took their seats, and several people stopped by their table to offer congratulations. When her face began to ache from smiling, she decided to take a break. "Excuse me. I need to powder my nose."

He stood as she rose, briefly putting his arm around her and sliding his mouth against her ear. "Don't get lost," he said and kissed her.

For just a moment, when his lips touched hers, the rest of the room disappeared, and she decided not to think about their arrangement. He felt so good that she decided not to think about the fact that this was a lie. Stealing an extra few seconds of his touch, she slid her hands up behind his neck and pressed into him.

He gave a low groan. "This is good, but…"

The flash of a camera snapped her out of her indulgence, and she pulled back. "Sorry. I guess I got into my role a little too much."

"It wasn't too much for me," he said.

She smiled and turned away. Maybe not too much for him, but was it too much for her? Instead of going to the powder room, she opted to walk down an empty hallway and take a breath. With each passing day, her feelings for Luc grew more intense. Passion was one thing, but what if she was really falling for him? What a horrible mistake that would be.

Standing in front of a window, she stared at the city lights blanketing the city and dotting the hills. She closed her eyes for a moment and thought of her house in Montana. She could practically feel the cold air on her cheeks, hear the crunch of frozen snow beneath her feet. A sense of peace trickled through her. She knew where she belonged.

"Gwen, it's you."

Her eyes blinked open at the sound of her ex-husband's voice, and she whirled toward him. "Peter," she said, looking into the face of the man she'd once thought she loved. "How are you?"

He gave a short, bitter laugh. "I could be better." He adjusted his tie and smoothed his hand over his hair. "I'm sure you've heard business hasn't been going smoothly for me since you left."

She took a step backward, wishing it were a mile. "I haven't kept up with things since I moved to Montana."

He gave a cryptic smile. "I thought you would grow tired of it. I heard you're involved with Luc Hudson. Pretty impressive. Bagged one of the big boys."

"He's good to me," she said.

"But he couldn't possibly be as good for you as I was.

We were in sync like no other," Peter said, moving closer. "We were set to take Hollywood by storm."

"Perhaps *you* were," she said, taking another step backward, feeling her foot collide with the wall.

"Gwen, you can't deny the synergy, the chemistry between us. It was amazing," he said.

She stopped him with her hand. "I remember it differently."

"We could have it again. I feel it right now. Don't you?"

She shook her head. "No, I—"

"Gwen."

Gwen turned her head, relieved at the sound of Luc's voice.

"You got lost powdering your nose," he joked, but his eyes were cold. He nodded in Peter's direction. "You'll have to excuse us. My fiancée is tired. She's had a long day."

Leading her away, Luc paged the driver on his Black-Berry. Within a moment of stepping outside, the limo appeared and Luc helped her inside. He climbed into the vehicle. "We'd like to go home," he said to the driver, then closed the privacy window and turned toward Gwen. "What the hell was that about?"

Eleven

"It was an ambush," she said. "I had no idea Peter was there. It wasn't intimate. It was creepy."

She sounded so sincere he almost relaxed. Then he remembered she was an actress, trained to lie. "It sure as hell looked intimate. I thought you were going to powder your nose."

"My cheeks hurt from forcing a smile. I'm out of practice," she said. "I needed a break."

"You should have told me that."

"In my way, I did tell you," she retorted.

"From the perspective of the press, it could have appeared that you were having some sort of lovers' rendezvous."

"And it's always about how it looks," she said, the bitterness in her voice taking him by surprise. "That's the way it was with Peter, too."

That stopped him. "What are you talking about?"

"It was no rendezvous, no glorious reunion. Peter was his usual pushy self, backing me against the wall before I realized it. He was always concerned about how I looked, how we appeared as a couple. Much more concerned with how I looked than who I was and what I needed," she said, her voice growing quiet. "It's the same with you. The only difference is that you're up-front about it."

He studied her for a long moment. "I don't like being compared to Peter Horrigan."

She looked out the window. "Maybe we should take a step ba—"

"No," he said, immediately rejecting the possibility. "We can't stop. There's something between us. It's been that way from the beginning."

She continued to stare out the window. "That's similar to what Peter said."

The notion nearly made him crazy. "Do you really think I'm like him?"

Gwen sighed and closed her eyes. "You're passionate and purposeful. You manipulate the media, but in some crazy way—" she said, opening her eyes and turning to look at him, "—you're more direct about it. Yes, you're demanding a performance from me, but it's for a specific goal with an end date." She shook her head. "It sounds crazy, but in a way, you blackmailed me, but you did it with my permission." She gave a reluctant half smile. "And you put your hot bachelor magazine spread the same place I put my sexiest woman feature."

He couldn't help chuckling. "In the trash can."

"Yeah. And Pyrrha seems to like you."

"That settles it. She would have hated Peter."

"Maybe not," Gwen said. "I think Pyrrha sensed that you would keep her safe."

He nodded, hearing a deeper message that had nothing to do with Pyrrha. "I can keep you safe, too, Gwen."

"Peter said the same thing, but when it came to a choice between my health, our baby's health and the movie he was making, he chose the movie."

Luc's face froze. "Baby," he echoed. "You were pregnant."

"That's why we divorced. He forced me to work sixteen-hour days to finish the movie before I started showing. There was an accident. I fell and had to be rushed to the hospital for emergency surgery. I lost the baby."

"Oh, sweetheart, I'm so sorry."

"I could never be in love with a man like that. I've never told anyone what happened, but I need you to know." She bit her lip. "This isn't just for show anymore. It's not just a fling."

"It never was a fling," he said. "I have no intention of stopping with you."

"We lead completely different lives in completely different places," she said.

"We'll deal with that when the time comes. Right now, we're together. I don't believe in wasting time," he said and took her mouth in a kiss.

The next few days, Gwen and Luc enjoyed staying out of the public eye by sticking close to Luc's bungalow.

His seemingly invisible chef prepared delicious dinners and dessert, which they enjoyed by candlelight on Luc's covered patio with an outdoor heater to keep them toasty warm.

Sitting in his lap as they watched the sunset, she almost liked being Luc's kept woman. "If we never had to go out, this wouldn't be half bad."

Luc chuckled. "Half bad. Don't inflate my ego anymore. It'll go to my head."

She gave him a light punch. "As if your ego needs any inflating. You're disgustingly self-confident." She waved her hand. "Look at your life, your house. All neatly arranged, no clutter, no messes."

"Because I clean up messes all day."

"I guess that's true," she said and met his gaze. "Then how is it that you can stand me? Between my sister and my life in Montana, I just add to your messes."

"Different kind of mess," he said. "By the way, I may have found a backer for your summer camp for disadvantaged children."

Surprised, she stared at him. "Really, who?"

"A contractor who's done a lot of work for us. He came up the hard way, but he's very successful now. He likes the idea of giving back."

"And how did you fit this in between reforming serial killers and ensuring that the next Hudson Pictures film gets phenomenal press?" she asked.

"Now you're trying to give me a big head," he said. The doorbell rang, and he gave a knowing glance. "You mind getting that?"

She paused, wondering what was behind the expression on his face. "Do you know who it is?"

"It's my driver with a delivery."

"What kind of delivery?"

"Why don't you go find out?"

Curious, she hopped out of his lap and went to the front door. She opened it and June leaped at her. "Oh, sweetie, how did you get here?"

The yellow Lab jumped up and made a whining noise that nearly broke Gwen's heart. "There you go. What a sweetheart. How did she get here?" she asked the driver.

"She flew," Luc said, coming from behind her and petting the dog.

"Flew? When?"

"Today. We needed to pick someone up from Minnesota and decided Montana was a good place to stop."

June wagged her tail in supreme pleasure and began to wander around the apartment. "She'll shed and drool on your perfect floors."

"That's why I have a cleaning lady."

Stunned by his thoughtfulness, she shook her head. "I don't know what to say except thank you."

"The look on your face is enough."

Gwen felt herself fall a little deeper for Luc. Knowing it couldn't end well terrified the living daylights out of her, so she tried not to think about the end and just enjoy the present.

Two days later, Gwen was forced to leave the bungalow in search of an evening gown for a big Valentine's Day bash to be held at Hudson Manor, the family estate in Beverly Hills. The estate was legendary. She'd been invited to a party there years ago, right after she'd lost her pregnancy, but she'd been unable to pull herself together for public viewing at the time. Peter had been furious with her.

Now she would see the estate through Luc's eyes and was looking forward to it. She looked through three stores before she found the perfect dress. She wanted to look spectacular for Luc, wanted him to feel proud of her and proud to be with her. She definitely, however, didn't want to think about what that meant.

After shopping she decided to stop by one of her favorite cafés to appease her grumbly stomach with soup and a sandwich. Relaxing at a corner table, she wore jeans, a T-shirt and a baseball cap, with her hair pulled back in a ponytail, to maintain a low profile.

Sipping her soup and chilled mint tea, she made a quick call to the ranch to check on the horses. Just as she wrapped up her call, Gwen glanced up to find Peter approaching her table.

Immediately rising, she shook her head, tightening her hand around her glass of mint tea. "I don't have anything else to say to you. Please leave me alone."

"Aw, Gwen, we have history. I just want a moment. Don't you think you owe me that much?"

"No," she said. "I don't owe you anything."

Peter looked from side to side. "Come on, Gwen, I'm the one who suffered after you left me. If you would come back for just one film," he began.

"Absolutely not," she said, furious that he would

even suggest it. "I told you I wanted a different life, and that's what I've made for myself."

"Do you really expect me to believe you won't be doing anything for Hudson Pictures?" he demanded and shook his head. "And your new fiancé. He's just riding on the coattails of his grandfather. I bet he hasn't worked a day in his life."

Her anger rose exponentially. "You have no idea how hard Luc works. He puts in a lot of hours behind the scenes."

"Wonder how many hours he has spent with you that were on the company clock," Peter said.

Infuriated, Gwen acted out of instinct and tossed her mint tea in his face. Peter looked at her in wet shock.

Disgusted with him and appalled at herself, she threw some money on the table, grabbed her dress and purse and fled the café. With trembling hands, she immediately called the driver as she walked quickly down the street. Although it felt like forever, he appeared beside her in mere moments.

The driver jumped out of the car and helped her get inside. "Are you okay? You look like you've seen a ghost," he said.

Gwen bit her lip and forced a laugh. "Is that what it was?"

"Seriously, we'll stop and get you something to eat. There's sparkling water and juice in the back, but no food."

Queasy from being taken by surprise by Peter, she shook her head. "No, just take me back to the bungalow please."

Within an hour of Gwen's return to the bungalow,

Luc showed up. He immediately found her in the office watching the horses. "What happened today?"

Still upset about the incident, she felt her stomach twist and turn. "I didn't want to bother you with it."

"What happened?"

Luc's tone only served to make her more nervous. She stood and took a breath. "Peter showed up when I was eating at a café."

Luc's expression turned to stone. "How did he know where you were?"

She shook her head. "I have no idea. It's almost as if he had a spy."

"What did he want?"

"He was trying to talk me into doing a movie with him. Then when he started to insult you, I just lost it," she said, anger rising inside her all over again.

Luc gave a sound of amused disgust. "What's he got on me?"

"He said you just ride your family's coattails," she said. "That made me so mad I threw my mint tea in his face."

Luc blinked. "You did what?"

"I know," she said, her emotions warring between extreme embarrassment and frustration. "It was impulsive and crazy and—"

"You didn't notice if there were any cameras around, did you?" he asked.

Dread sank into her. "Oh, no." She covered her face. "I didn't see anyone, but I guess that doesn't mean anything. I was so fried I'm not sure I would have noticed." She slowly dropped her hands, grimacing. "I'm sorry."

He chuckled. "Don't worry. It could be worse."

Relief shot through her as he pulled her against him. "I'm not sure how."

"Sure it could," he said. "You acted like an angry, protective fiancée. If you're not careful, I may start to believe you myself."

On February 14th, Gwen dressed in her new teal gown with a slit and walked into Luc's living room, where he was talking on his cell phone. His jaw dropped and he looked her over from head to toe.

"I need to go. I'll talk to you later," he said and turned off the phone. He stared at her for a long moment. "I'm speechless. You look amazing."

Others had paid her compliments and told her she was beautiful, but no one else had made her heart stop like Luc did. "Thank you."

"I've seen you in photographs. I've seen your movies. But something about you is different than it used to be. You just seem more real."

Thrilled that he not only saw it but could also name it, she nodded. "I am. I weigh a few pounds more than I did. I will sacrifice only so much for the sake of beauty these days. I don't like pretending."

He skimmed his finger over her shoulder, making the strap fall down her arm. "It's a damn shame I have to take you out tonight. I'd much rather keep you here," he said, sliding his arm around her waist.

"But family and duty call, and answering those calls is just part of who you are," she said.

"You don't resent it," he mused.

"How can I? When you got the call about Nicki, you took care of her immediately."

"I have to tell you my first response when I answered the phone was anger that she had gotten herself into this mess. When I saw her, though, she just looked like a mixed-up kid."

"And you had to help her," she said. "That white knight thing."

"That's a myth," he said.

"Not from my experience. Pyrrha could tattle on you, too."

"Enough," he said with a groan. "The sooner we go, the sooner I can bring you back here and have you to myself."

Luc escorted her outside and into the limo, then told the driver they were ready. "I don't know how much you know about Hudson Manor."

"I was once invited to an event there, but I couldn't attend."

"Is that so?" he said more than asked and rubbed his chin. "Hudson Manor was built by my grandfather for my grandmother."

The stone and wrought-iron mansion that was built on acres of land on Loma Vista Drive in Beverly Hills was legendary. "That's a pretty big statement of love and devotion."

"My grandfather did things in a big way," Luc said.

"You miss him," she said, hearing it in his voice.

"Yeah, he was something else. But if I get quiet and think about him, I can hear him laugh and smell his cigar."

"You're so lucky to have that kind of family connection," she said.

He skimmed his finger down her cheek. "And you miss it," he concluded.

Her stomach twisted. "Yes, I do." She took a quick breath. "Who will be there tonight?"

He chuckled. "It's easier to tell you who won't be there."

"Okay, then who won't be?"

"My uncle David. He's in Europe producing and directing an independent film. He doesn't come around much anyway."

"Why not?"

Luc shrugged. "His wife died a long time ago and he sent his son, Jack, to live with my grandmother and grandfather. He's disconnected from the rest of the family, and it looks like that's the way he wants it."

Gwen shook her head, unable to imagine why someone would deliberately choose to be disconnected from a loving family. "That's a shame."

"Yeah, it is. But you'll get to meet everyone else."

"I was actually introduced to Max, Devlin and your father before," she said.

"How did you meet them without meeting me?"

"It was some big industry event. As soon as Peter saw me talking to members of your family, he whisked me away. He was very controlling about who I was exposed to."

"That surprises me," Luc said. "You strike me as a very independent-minded woman."

"Now," she said, remembering those days when she'd felt insecure and willing to sacrifice anything to please Peter. "It took me a while to trust myself."

"Now you're Superwoman, rescuing horses and throwing glasses of tea in the face of villains."

She rolled her eyes. "One glass of tea," she corrected. "I won't make it a habit."

The limo pulled into a long driveway, distracting her from her irritation. It wove its way to the front of the mansion, dramatically illuminated by floodlights.

"Oh, wow."

"My grandmother said something similar when my grandfather showed her the completed building. They spent years furnishing it. It always amazed me that they managed to make such a grand place feel like home."

"I can't wait for you to give me a tour," she said and kissed his cheek.

"My pleasure."

Luc led Gwen from the limo up the steps to the front door, where a stout woman with gray hair greeted them.

"Hannah," he said to the longtime Hudson family housekeeper and gave her a hug. "How did you get stuck with the late shift tonight?"

"I asked for it," she said. "I knew just about everyone would be coming tonight, and I wanted to see all of you." She glanced at Gwen, sizing her up. "Who's this pretty woman you have with you tonight?"

"Gwen McCord," he said. "She's my fiancée."

Hannah's eyes widened. "Is she now? I thought it would be a long time before you settled down."

"She changed my mind," he said, looking at Gwen and feeling more as if he could be telling the truth than playing a game.

"Well, then," Hannah said. "You must be some woman."

"I'm working on it," Gwen said and extended her hand. "It's nice to meet you."

"Have I heard your name before?" Hannah asked, her brow furrowing.

"Perhaps," Gwen said. "I did a couple of movies, but I'm out of the business now."

"Hmm," Hannah said, then turned to Luc. "Nice to see you with someone closer to your age."

"I hear you," Luc said and led Gwen inside. He took the French provincial decor, marble floors and hand-painted wallpaper of his family home for granted, but he suspected Gwen didn't when he heard her gasp.

"Oh, my goodness," she said, looking around. "Does anyone actually live here?"

Luc nodded. "My grandmother has private quarters on the first floor. My father and mother live on the second floor in the left wing. Dev has the second floor, right wing, and Bella moved to the guesthouse a few years ago."

"You must have felt like you'd gone camping when you arrived at my little cabin," Gwen said.

"Not really. Aside from all the pink in the guest room," he added with a sideways glance.

"I was trying to get you to leave," she confessed.

"It would have taken more than pink draperies and a bunch of knickknacks to send me running."

"You surprised me," she said. "More than once."

The expression in her eyes grabbed at his gut and made him start thinking crazy things, such as how to make their relationship last past the end of February.

Twelve

"Luc, darling. I feel like I haven't seen you in ages," a handsome middle-aged woman said. "And I hear your grandmother is going to make an announcement in just a few minutes."

Luc kissed the woman on her cheek. "Hi, Mom. I'd like you to meet Gwen McCord."

The woman extended her hand to Gwen. "Lovely. I'm Sabrina. Pleased to meet you." She picked up Gwen's left hand and examined the engagement ring. "Excellent taste. I just wish it were real."

"The diamond is quite real," Luc said.

"You know what I mean," Sabrina said.

"It's nice to meet you," Gwen said. "Your home is so lovely."

Sabrina looked around and smiled. "Charles did right by Lillian. He was crazy about her until the day he died."

Several men walked up behind Sabrina.

"The natives are curious," Luc said under his breath. "My father and brothers."

"Gwen McCord," a tall, distinguished man said, extending his hand. "You may not remember, but we met once before."

Gwen saw the family resemblance in Luc and the other males in his family. "Of course I remember you, Mr. Hudson," she said, shaking his hand. "We met at the Red Cross charity gala. I also met Devlin and Max."

"Good memory," Devlin, Luc's eldest brother, said. "Just don't give her anything to drink when I'm around. I don't want to end up with it in my face."

Gwen winced. "How did you hear about that?"

"It's on the Internet," Devlin said. "I need to get back to my date before she runs screaming."

"Who's the unlucky woman?" Luc asked.

Devlin threw Luc a quelling glance. "Valerie Shelton. Be nice to her," he said and walked away.

"Whoa," Luc said.

"They're dating," his mother said with a sigh. "But she's very shy, very sweet. She just seems so vulnerable. I'm not sure how long it will last. Devlin has such a strong personality. I'm not sure she'll be able to…"

Her husband cleared his throat. "They're both adults," he reminded her.

"True, and I would love some grandchildren."

"There are a few steps to go before that happens," Mr. Hudson said.

Another Hudson brother, tall with dark hair and insightful blue eyes, extended his hand. "Hi, I'm Max. I'm the producer for the movie *The Waiting Room*. I appreciate you—" He paused a half beat. "Stepping up after your sister's difficulty."

Her stomach twisted. His reference, albeit delicate, to the faux engagement reminded her that ultimately this was all business for the Hudsons. She nodded and decided not to comment. "It's good to meet you again."

"I'm surprised you remembered. You'd just received your Oscar nomination and were swarmed that night. Speaking of which, I've admired your work. If you're interested in doing anything with Hudson Pictures, give me a call."

"Thanks, but I'm very busy in Montana right now. I've admired your work, too. Your last thriller was fabulous."

Luc slid his arm around her waist. "We should go inside. Can't keep our grandmother waiting when she has something to announce. She's got me curious."

Luc led Gwen into a grand parlor full of beautifully dressed women and men wearing tuxes. Lillian Colbert Hudson stood in the center of the room. Like an elderly queen addressing her subjects, she stood with a regal beauty despite her advanced age. Her auburn hair contrasted vividly with her shimmering gown.

"She's amazing," Gwen said. "I've seen photographs of her and some of her films, but I've never seen her in person."

Luc nodded. "She's growing more frail, but she's still sharp. Not much gets past her."

Luc's father tapped a crystal glass with a sterling silver

spoon and silence descended over the room. Lillian smiled at him. "Thank you, dear." She turned her attention to the roomful of people. "Happy Valentine's Day," she said, her smile growing broader and her eyes twinkling.

A few chuckles echoed through the crowd.

"As you know, my sweetheart, the love of my life, was Charles Hudson. We met during World War II in France. He was a dashing American, and I was a young cabaret singer in a nightclub. Both of us were fighting against the Germans, although we didn't know it until Charles was injured and I hid him in my tiny apartment.

"We secretly married." Lillian smiled. "No big wedding, which is part of the reason I enjoy all of your weddings. When France was liberated, Charles was sent to Germany. He promised he would come for me. I would have waited forever for that man, but thank God I didn't have to. He brought me to America and made me the happiest woman in the world. I can only wish that kind of love for all of you.

"It was always his dream that our love story be commemorated in the form of a film. The time has never been more right for this project than with the sixtieth diamond anniversary of Hudson Pictures." Lillian took a breath that created a dramatic pause. "I'm very pleased to announce that our story will indeed be told in the motion picture entitled *Honor*. Thank you in advance to all of you for your contributions to this project that is so close to my heart and will honor the memory of our much-loved Charles."

Seeing the obvious love on Lillian's face brought tears to Gwen's eyes. Her mind turned to her own overwhelming feelings for Luc, and she wondered again what would eventually happen between them.

Feeling his gaze on her, she couldn't keep from looking at him. His eyes glimmered with the same emotion she felt, and he raised his finger to catch a tear. "You okay?"

"What an incredible love they must have shared," she said.

He nodded. "They found the right person in the middle of terrible circumstances and didn't let go."

Was it possible that the same kind of love was developing between her and Luc? Was she crazy to think so? Luc slid his hand down to take hers, twining his fingers through hers. "Would you like to meet her?"

Gwen nodded. "Yes, of course."

Luc threaded through the crowd around Lillian, waving to get her attention. She smiled and stepped toward him.

"It's so good to see you, darling," Lillian said. "I don't see you often enough. Now introduce me to your Gwen McCord."

Shocked that Lillian recognized her, she swallowed a gasp.

"Can't slip anything past you." Luc chuckled and gave his grandmother an affectionate hug. "Grandmother, Lillian Hudson, this is Gwen McCord."

Lillian took Gwen's hand and looked into her eyes. "You have a good heart. I can see it. I also saw one of your movies. You were lovely."

"Thank you, Mrs. Hudson. I'm very honored to meet you."

Lillian glanced meaningfully at the diamond on Gwen's left hand. "You and my grandson are close."

Gwen stole a quick glance at Luc and nodded. "It's a little complicated."

Lillian nodded. "Some of the best things start out that way. I speak from experience. I hope to see you again," she said and was whisked away by another guest.

"Thank you," Gwen said, knowing she would always treasure meeting Lillian.

"My pleasure," Luc said. "Would you like something to drink?"

"I would love some sparkling water," Gwen said.

"No wine even though you're not on duty tonight?" he asked.

"Look what happened with tea," she said wryly.

"Will you be okay alone?"

"Fine," she said. "It will give me a chance to gawk at the beautiful furnishings."

Luc headed for the bar at the back of the room, waving to family members and friends as he made his way there. He got a glass of red wine for himself and sparkling water with lime for Gwen.

"I see you brought your new fiancée," his cousin Jack said as he ordered a glass of Patrón.

"Yes, I did," Luc said, glancing across the room at Gwen as she studied a collection of Fabergé eggs in a display. "She's even more beautiful in person than she was on the screen."

Jack nodded and took a swallow of his drink. "Your engagement is convincing. Looks like the two of you have gotten close. Not a bad bonus if you ask 98 percent of the men in this room."

Luc shook his head. "I figured she was like every other actress I've met. Self-centered, high-maintenance, a climber. From the first moment I met her, she was different."

"By that, you mean different in a good way," Jack said.

"For the most part," Luc said, thinking that her stubbornness matched his own. "What about you? Will you be working on Charles and Lillian's movie?"

"Grandmother has asked me to get a screenwriter on board right away. She has a preference for Cheryl Cassidy."

"She's good," Luc said.

"Yes, she is. The only problem is she won't speak to me."

"Why not?" Luc asked, surprised.

"She and I were once involved."

"Must have been a helluva breakup," Luc said.

"It wasn't pretty," Jack agreed.

Luc patted his cousin on the back. "Good luck."

"Thanks," Jack said.

Bella zipped between both of them. "Champagne," she said to the bartender. "Isn't this exciting? Everyone should be drinking champagne and toasting. I want to be in this movie," she said.

"You and only three thousand other actresses," Max said from behind Luc. "Get in line."

Bella scowled. "Thanks for your support."

"I'm just telling it like it is," Max said and glanced at Luc and Jack. "Am I right?"

"Unfortunately," Jack said.

"There's no reason you shouldn't get a shot at it," Luc said.

"Except for the fact that I'm a Hudson, and Hudsons are twice as hard on their own as anyone else." She tossed her auburn hair. "No problem. I'm willing to work twice as hard and twice as long."

As she whipped around and strode away, Luc looked at his brother and cousin. "I'd say she just told us."

"Can't agree more," Max said with a chuckle.

"I'll leave the two of you to the bar. I have a beautiful woman waiting for me on the other side of the room."

Max shook his head. "Still surprised you fell for her. She's not your usual type at all."

"That's part of the draw," Luc said but refused to say any more. Despite the publicity surrounding his relationship, Luc felt a deep sense of privacy about his feelings for Gwen. The feelings they shared were between the two of them and no one else.

After the big Valentine's Day bash, Gwen was caught between a state of euphoria and one of falling off a cliff. She e-mailed Nicki and took June for walks while Luc went to work; they shared their nights together. He told her about how he set up an individual strategy for each actor, each role and each film. Although she'd known PR played a tremendous role in the promotion of films, she'd never realized the intense analysis that went into the overall plan. In her experience, she'd just always done whatever she was told to do.

She and Luc attended a prerelease publicity event for

The Waiting Room. Gwen was quizzed about throwing tea in the face of her ex-husband, and Luc simply said, "She was defending my honor."

The reporter laughed and Gwen plugged *The Waiting Room* as assigned. Later that night Luc made delicious love to Gwen. Afterward, she lay curled against him with one of his arms holding her close to the front of him.

This was bliss, she realized. Total and complete bliss. With Luc, she felt free and protected, encouraged and supported, yet challenged, too.

She had never felt more at home than in his arms.

Realization reverberated through her like an earthquake. Gwen had fallen in love with Luc.

The next morning she awakened to the sensation of Luc kissing the back of her neck. She couldn't help but smile.

"Tickles," she said in a voice that sounded sleep-husky to her own ears.

Luc slid his hand upward to her breast, toying with the nipple, making her gasp. "Tickles?" he asked in a taunting voice.

"In a different way," she said.

Within moments, he was touching her intimately, making her wet and needy, thrusting inside her. He took her up to the top and over, then followed after.

"I love," he said, making her heart catch with those words. "Having you in my bed."

She took a deep breath while trying to clear her head, but it was tough with her brain still scrambled from amazing sex and Luc's arms still around her.

"I want to keep you around," he said in a growly voice that rippled up her nerve endings.

"How do you plan to do that?"

"Gotta give you a challenge, and I've found one," he said. "Hudson Pictures is producing a film about a martyred peace worker. It's the perfect comeback role for Gwen McCord."

Still emerging from the fog of a delicious afterglow, she tried to concentrate. "Comeback role?" she echoed.

"Yes," he said, turning her over so that she faced him. "It will be filmed mostly in California. That way we could be together."

Gwen wrinkled her brow and shook her head. "But I don't want to come back," she told him. "I like what I'm doing in Montana. It feels right for me."

"You can still visit Montana," he said, skimming his finger down her cheek. "Think it over. Just remember, it will give us a chance to be together more." He brushed his mouth over hers. "I haven't had enough of you. Damn it, I wish I didn't have to go to work now," he said but appeared to force himself out of bed.

He took a quick shower, dressed and grabbed another kiss. Then he was out the door. Slowly gathering her wits, Gwen sat up in the bed and pulled the sheets up with her. The prospect of another movie role left her with a chill.

She shivered as chill bumps surfaced on her skin. Frowning, she tried to comprehend why Luc had discussed the role with her. Had he truly not understood that she had no interest in returning to the movie business?

Or worse, was this another example of manipulation? Had Luc seduced her so that she would accept a role with Hudson Pictures?

The prospect sliced through her like a knife. She couldn't believe it was possible, yet the thought lingered like a ghost.

She got out of bed, tried to shower the darkness out of her and went to view her horses on Luc's laptop. Watching them made her realize how much she'd missed being in Montana. Being where she belonged.

She needed to go back. The decision snapped inside her. She didn't know what would happen between her and Luc, but her commitment to the faux engagement had been over after Valentine's Day. Technically, she could have left then, but she'd dallied. With Luc it had been so easy to dally.

As she began to pack, she called Luc, but her call was put straight through to voice mail. Reluctant to leave a message, she tried repeatedly. She finally called his assistant, but that call, too, was put through to voice mail.

Troubled but determined, she wrote a note and called a cab. Packing her small suitcase and leaving the glamorous dresses Luc had bought for her in the closet, she took off the engagement ring and placed it on the dresser.

Then she walked out of his bungalow into the waiting cab that would take her to the airport.

Following a day of crisis, Luc arrived home after seven o'clock. An actor from an upcoming feature film had been arrested for domestic abuse by his wife of three years. Luc knew that often people considered him a miracle worker, but there were some things he couldn't fix. In this case, there were some things he didn't want to fix.

He and his assistant had been on the phone all day

trying to get treatment for the actor and provide a safe place for his wife and children.

On days like this he was ready to move to Montana with Gwen. She wouldn't need to ask twice.

Stepping inside his bungalow, he waited for June to greet him with a bark and a wagging tail. Gwen would follow with open arms.

Instead, silence greeted him. Surprised, Luc moved through his house. "Gwen? Where are you?"

He passed his office and approached the laptop on the desk. It was turned off. Frowning, he paced through the other rooms, finally walking into his bedroom. There, he saw a ring on his dresser and what looked like a note.

A ball of dread formed in his gut. He approached the dresser and picked the ring up in one hand and the note in the other.

Dear Luc, I had to go home. I was losing touch with who I am and who I want to be. As much as I loved my time with you, I don't want to go back to the Hollywood lifestyle. I am forever grateful for how you helped my sister. You deserve every good thing. Always, Gwen.

Gone, he realized. Was she really gone? Hadn't he held her in his arms just this morning? Hadn't he made love to her just before he left?

His gut churned and his chest hurt. Luc felt as if his world had been turned upside down.

Gone, he realized. Why hadn't she called him? Why had she left that blasted note? She should have at least given him a chance to talk with her. He deserved that much. They deserved that much.

The ring felt cold in his palm. Setting it back on the

dresser, he sank down on the bed. He'd grown accustomed to having her in his bed. Worse yet, he'd grown accustomed to having her in his life.

This wasn't a fake relationship or fake anything anymore. What he felt for Gwen was completely real.

Epilogue

Three days later, Gwen finished mucking out the stalls and stopped by Pyrrha's stall before she faced temperatures in the single digits. Part of her had felt pure relief as she'd driven into the long driveway to her house. She and June had bounded into the cold snow and skipped around the yard.

After tossing her luggage into the house, she'd raced to the stables to reacquaint herself with the horses, the smell of fresh hay and the sense of quiet contentment her rescue efforts provided her.

None of this stopped her from missing Luc. The sharp longing she felt upon rising and going to bed stunned her, but she ignored his repeated calls. She kept telling herself that he represented everything she wanted to leave behind—the false front of Hollywood, the fast pace, the concern about appearances.

But she knew better. Luc was more than that. He did what he did for his family and for the heritage of his grandparents. His family depended on him because he was a problem solver extraordinaire. They were right. Look what he'd done for her sister, Nicki. Gwen had been in touch with Nicki daily, and she was due to leave the rehab center any day.

Nicki was nervous but more purposeful. She'd grown up and decided to go after her happiness. No more self-medication. Nicki was ready to take care of herself, and she knew she could call Gwen at any time to be by her side. Gwen had a strong feeling that Nicki would make it, and she had Luc to thank for that.

Another longing spurted through her, spreading throughout her bloodstream, permeating her. Heaven help her, this trying to get over Luc sucked in a big way.

Plus, there was the tiny matter of the calendar and the fact that Gwen was late. Very late.

Gwen tried to close her eyes to the possibility, but when she looked at Pyrrha, she couldn't help but wonder if she and the mare were suddenly in the same family way.

Gwen sighed and the horse sauntered toward her and nodded at her. A little thrill raced through her at the horse's increasing trust.

"You're getting there, aren't you, girl?" she whispered.

Hearing footsteps, Gwen glanced behind her, and her heart stopped at the sight of Luc walking toward her.

"Bet you thought you got rid of me, sneaking out like that," he said, swaggering toward her.

Her heart began to beat again, this time in her throat. She gulped. "I didn't sneak."

He raised a dark eyebrow. "No?"

"No," she said. "I didn't. I called you several times, but you didn't pick up."

"Because I was dealing with an actor accused of domestic abuse," he said.

"Oh," she said, grimacing. "I tried your assistant too, but—"

"She was working on the same situation."

Gwen took a deep breath to clear her head and ease the tight feeling in her chest. A ball of emotion formed in her throat and hung there. She felt herself sinking into Luc's blue eyes.

"What made you leave?"

Gwen bit her lip. "It terrified me when you mentioned that film role. It reminded me of Peter pressuring me to take a role to build his business, even though deep inside I knew you weren't trying to do that. I couldn't stop the old feelings, and I realized I desperately needed to feel grounded again. I needed to come back home, and home for me is here."

Luc gave a slow nod. "Do you have room for someone else in your home?"

Her heart seemed to stop again. "What do you mean?"

"I mean," he said, moving close to her, "do you have room in your home for me?"

Gwen felt as if she could faint. Locking her knees, she swallowed hard and took a deep breath. "Yes, I do."

"Why?" he demanded, placing his hand on her face. "Why do you have room for me?"

"Because I'm in love with you," Gwen whispered without hesitation.

"That's damn good to know," Luc said, pulling her against him. "Would you be open to sharing two residences?"

"Do I have to do movies?"

"Never ever," Luc said.

"Yes," she said, wondering if she were dreaming. "I can't believe you came after me."

"I can't believe you doubted that I would do anything else," Luc said. "You and I, we've found something special. You know my family history. Once we meet that special someone, nothing will stop us."

She closed her eyes, trying to take it all in. "I don't know what to say."

"Say you'll marry me," he said, rubbing his cheek against hers.

Her eyes flashed open. "Are you serious?"

"I couldn't be more so," he said and sank down on one knee before her. "Gwen McCord, I love you, heart and soul. Will you marry me and be my wife?"

Her chest squeezed tight, and her eyes filled with tears. "Oh, Luc."

"Say yes," he said.

She took another quick breath. "I feel as if I should tell you something," she said. "I think I may be pregnant."

His jaw dropped and he rose. "Pregnant? Are you sure?"

"Pretty sure. I'm late and I've had symptoms since I was in California, but I haven't taken a test yet."

He stared at her in wonder. "Nothing in the world

would make me happier than having a baby with you. Except just living the rest of my life with you."

"Oh, Luc, I love you so very much. I never knew what love really was until I met you."

"You make me feel like I've come home," he said. "I've been looking for you my entire life but didn't know it until I found you."

Gwen stretched her arms around him and pushed her face against his jaw. "Let's get started," she said. "With the rest of our lives."

* * * * *

Don't miss TEMPTED INTO THE TYCOON'S TRAP
by Emily McKay,
the next HUDSONS OF BEVERLY HILLS,
available in February 2009 from Silhouette Desire.

'I've found her.'

Max froze.

It was what he'd been waiting for since June, but now—now he was almost afraid to voice the question. His heart stalling, he leaned slowly back in his chair and scoured the investigator's face for clues. 'Where?' he asked, and his voice sounded rough and unused, like a rusty hinge.

'In Suffolk. She's living in a cottage.'

Living. His heart crashed back to life, and he sucked in a long, slow breath. All these months he'd feared—

'Is she well?'

'Yes, she's well.'

He had to force himself to ask the next question. 'Alone?'

The man paused. 'No. The cottage belongs to a man called John Blake. He's working away at the moment, but he comes and goes.'

God. He felt sick. So sick he hardly registered the next few words, but then gradually they sank in. 'She's got *what?*'

'Babies. Twin girls. They're eight months old.'

'Eight—?' he echoed under his breath. 'They must be his.'

He was thinking out loud, but the P.I. heard and corrected him.

'Apparently not. I gather they're hers. She's been there since mid-January last year, and they were born during the summer—June, the woman in the post office thought. She was more than helpful. I think there's been a certain amount of speculation about their relationship.'

He'd just bet there had. God, he was going to kill her. Or Blake. Maybe both of them.

'Of course, looking at the dates, she was presumably pregnant when she left you, so they could be yours, or she could have been having an affair with this Blake character before…'

He glared at the unfortunate P.I. 'Just stick to your job. I can do the math,' he snapped, swallowing the unpalatable possibility that she'd been unfaithful to him before she'd left. 'Where is she? I want the address.'

'It's all in here,' the man said, sliding a large envelope across the desk to him. 'With my invoice.'

'I'll get it seen to. Thank you.'

'If there's anything else you need, Mr Gallagher, any further information—'

'I'll be in touch.'

'The woman in the post office told me Blake was away at the moment, if that helps,' he added quietly, and opened the door.

Max stared down at the envelope, hardly daring to open it, but when the door clicked softly shut behind the P.I., he eased up the flap, tipped it and felt his breath jam in his throat as the photos spilled out over the desk.

Oh, lord, she looked gorgeous. Different, though. It took him a moment to recognise her, because she'd grown her hair, and it was tied back in a ponytail, making her look younger and somehow freer. The blond highlights were gone, and it was back to its natural soft golden-brown, with a little curl in the end of the ponytail that he wanted to thread his finger through and tug, just gently, to draw her back to him.

Crazy. She'd put on a little weight, but it suited her. She looked well and happy and beautiful, but oddly, considering how desperate he'd been for news of her for the past year—one year, three weeks and two days, to be exact—it wasn't only Julia who held his attention after the initial shock. It was the babies sitting side by side in a supermarket trolley. Two identical and absolutely beautiful little girls.

* * * * *

When Max Gallagher hires a P.I. to find his estranged wife, Julia, he discovers she's not alone—she has twin baby girls, and they might be his. Now workaholic Max has just two weeks to prove that he can be a wonderful husband and father to the family he wants to treasure.

Look for TWO LITTLE MIRACLES
by Caroline Anderson,
available February 2009 from Harlequin Romance®.

CELEBRATE
60 YEARS
OF PURE READING PLEASURE
WITH **HARLEQUIN**®!

We'll be spotlighting a different series
every month throughout 2009
to celebrate our 60th anniversary.

Look for Harlequin® Romance in February!

**Harlequin® Romance is celebrating by showering
you with Diamond Brides in February 2009.**

Six stories that promise to bring a touch of sparkle to
your life, with diamond proposals and dazzling weddings,
sparkling brides and gorgeous grooms!

Collect all six books in February 2009,
featuring *Two Little Miracles* by Caroline Anderson.

*Look for the Diamond Brides miniseries
in February 2009!*

www.eHarlequin.com   HRBRIDES09

HARLEQUIN® Romance®

This February the Harlequin® Romance series
will feature six Diamond Brides stories featuring
diamond proposals and gorgeous grooms.

Share your dream wedding proposal and you could WIN!

The most romantic entry will win a diamond
necklace and will inspire a proposal in one of
our upcoming Diamond Grooms books in 2010.

In 100 words or less, tell us the most romantic
way that you dream of being proposed to.

For more information, and to enter
the Diamond Brides Proposal contest, please visit
www.DiamondBridesProposal.com

Or mail your entry to us at:

IN THE U.S.: 3010 Walden Ave., P.O. Box 9069, Buffalo, NY 14269-9069
IN CANADA: 225 Duncan Mill Road, Don Mills, ON M3B 3K9

REQUEST YOUR FREE BOOKS!

2 FREE NOVELS PLUS 2 FREE GIFTS!

Silhouette® Desire®

Passionate, Powerful, Provocative!

YES! Please send me 2 FREE Silhouette Desire® novels and my 2 FREE gifts (gifts are worth about $10). After receiving them, if I don't wish to receive any more books, I can return the shipping statement marked "cancel". If I don't cancel, I will receive 6 brand-new novels every month and be billed just $4.05 per book in the U.S. or $4.74 per book in Canada, plus 25¢ shipping and handling per book and applicable taxes, if any*. That's a savings of almost 15% off the cover price! I understand that accepting the 2 free books and gifts places me under no obligation to buy anything. I can always return a shipment and cancel at any time. Even if I never buy another book, the two free books and gifts are mine to keep forever.   225 SDN ERVX 326 SDN ERVM

Name _____ (PLEASE PRINT) _____

Address _____ Apt. # _____

City _____ State/Prov. _____ Zip/Postal Code _____

Signature (if under 18, a parent or guardian must sign)

Mail to the **Silhouette Reader Service:**
IN U.S.A.: P.O. Box 1867, Buffalo, NY 14240-1867
IN CANADA: P.O. Box 609, Fort Erie, Ontario L2A 5X3

Not valid to current subscribers of Silhouette Desire books.

Want to try two free books from another line?
Call 1-800-873-8635 or visit www.morefreebooks.com.

* Terms and prices subject to change without notice. N.Y. residents add applicable sales tax. Canadian residents will be charged applicable provincial taxes and GST. Offer not valid in Quebec. This offer is limited to one order per household. All orders subject to approval. Credit or debit balances in a customer's account(s) may be offset by any other outstanding balance owed by or to the customer. Please allow 4 to 6 weeks for delivery. Offer available while quantities last.

Your Privacy: Silhouette Books is committed to protecting your privacy. Our Privacy Policy is available online at www.eHarlequin.com or upon request from the Reader Service. From time to time we make our lists of customers available to reputable third parties who may have a product or service of interest to you. If you would prefer we not share your name and address, please check here. ☐

SDES08R

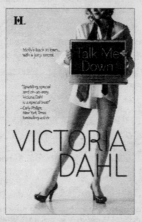

COMING NEXT MONTH

#1921 MR. STRICTLY BUSINESS—Day Leclaire
Man of the Month
He'd always taken what he wanted, when he wanted it—but she
wouldn't bend to those rules. Now she needs his help. His price?
Her—back in his bed.

#1922 TEMPTED INTO THE TYCOON'S TRAP—
Emily McKay
The Hudsons of Beverly Hills
When he finds out that her secret baby is really his, he demands
that she marry him. But their passion hasn't fizzled, and soon their
marriage of convenience becomes very real.

#1923 CONVENIENT MARRIAGE, INCONVENIENT
HUSBAND—Yvonne Lindsay
Rogue Diamonds
She'd left him at the altar eight years ago, but now she needs him
in order to gain her inheritance. Could this be his chance to teach
her that one can't measure love with money?

#1924 RESERVED FOR THE TYCOON—Charlene Sands
Suite Secrets
His new events planner is trying to sabotage his hotel, but his
attraction to her is like nothing he's ever felt. Will he choose to
destroy her...or seduce her?

#1925 MILLIONAIRE'S SECRET SEDUCTION—
Jennifer Lewis
The Hardcastle Progeny
On discovering a beautiful woman's intentions to sue his father's
company, he makes her a deal—her body in exchange for his
silence.

#1926 THE C.O.O. MUST MARRY—Maxine Sullivan
Their fathers forced them to marry each other to save their
families' fortunes. Will a former young love blossom again, or
will secrets drive them apart?

SDCNMBPA0109